The Mystery Monster

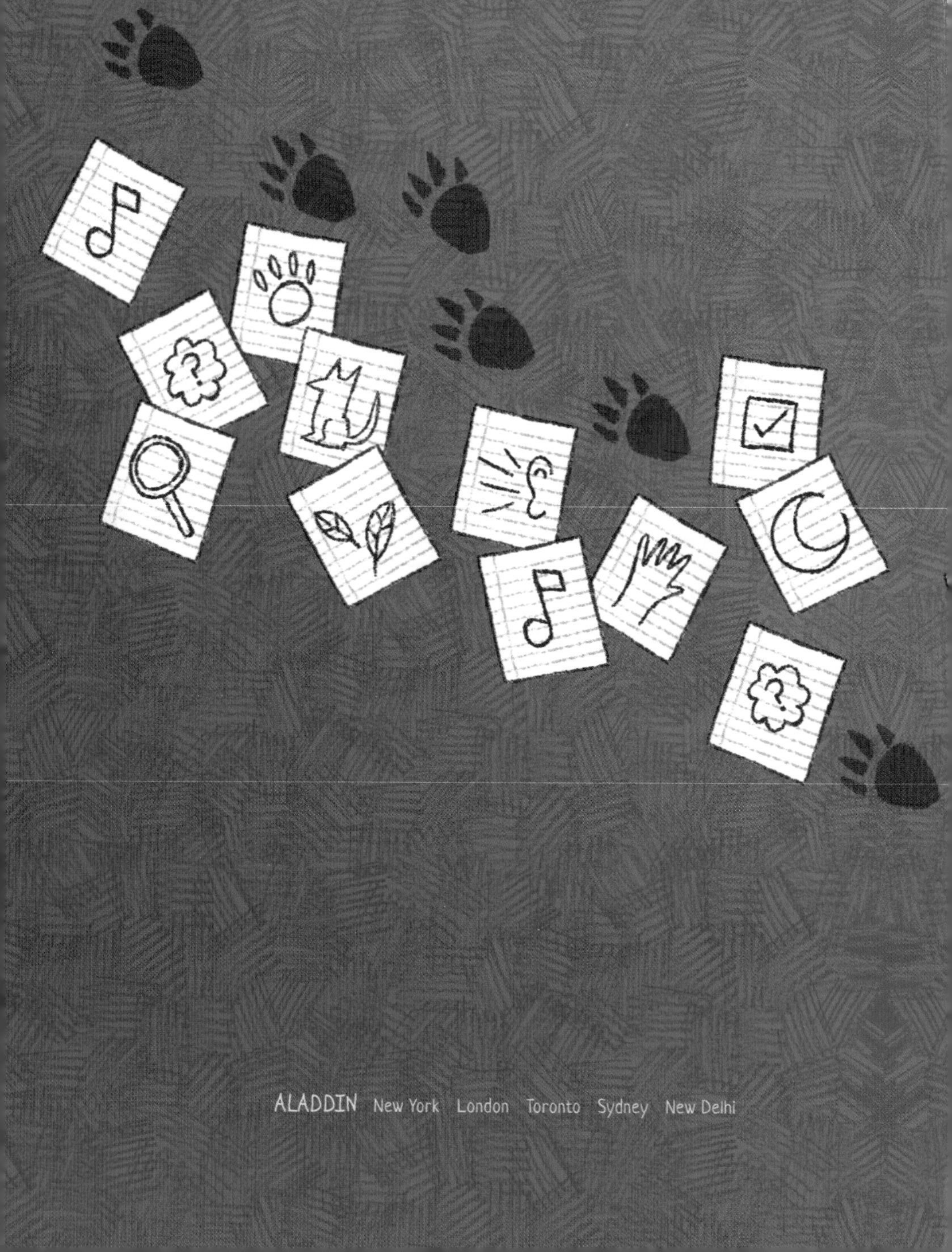

ALADDIN New York London Toronto Sydney New Delhi

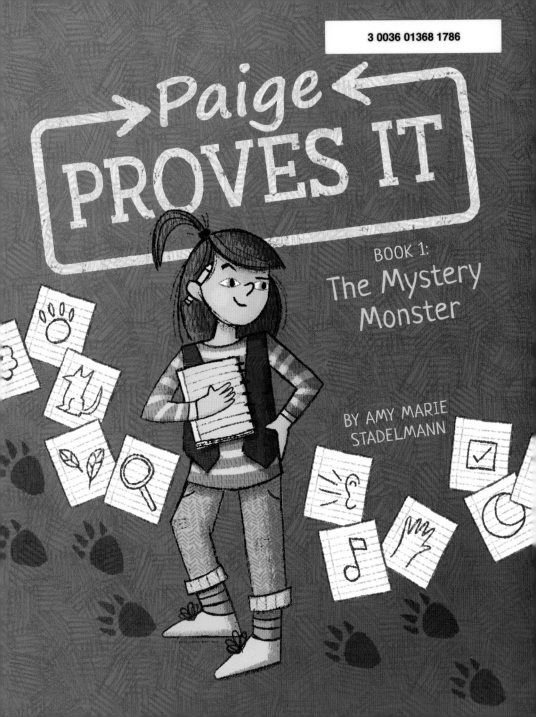

Paige
PROVES IT

BOOK 1:
The Mystery
Monster

BY AMY MARIE
STADELMANN

ALADDIN
An imprint of Simon & Schuster Children's Publishing Division
1230 Avenue of the Americas, New York, New York 10020
First Aladdin hardcover edition June 2021
Text copyright © 2021 by Amy Marie Stadelmann
Cover illustration copyright © 2021 by Amy Marie Stadelmann
Interior illustrations copyright © 2021 Amy Marie Stadelmann
All rights reserved, including the right of reproduction in whole or in part in any form.
ALADDIN and related logo are registered trademarks of Simon & Schuster, Inc.
For information about special discounts for bulk purchases, please contact Simon & Schuster Special Sales at 1-866-506-1949 or business@simonandschuster.com.
The Simon & Schuster Speakers Bureau can bring authors to your live event. For more information or to book an event contact the Simon & Schuster Speakers Bureau at 1-866-248-3049 or visit our website at www.simonspeakers.com.
Book designed by Tiara Iandiorio
The illustrations for this book were rendered in pencil and digitally colored.
The text of this book was set in Austral Slab.
Manufactured in China 0321 SCP
10 9 8 7 6 5 4 3 2 1
This book has been cataloged with the Library of Congress.
ISBN 978-1-5344-5161-2 (hc)
ISBN 978-1-5344-5160-5 (pbk)
ISBN 978-1-5344-5162-9 (eBook)

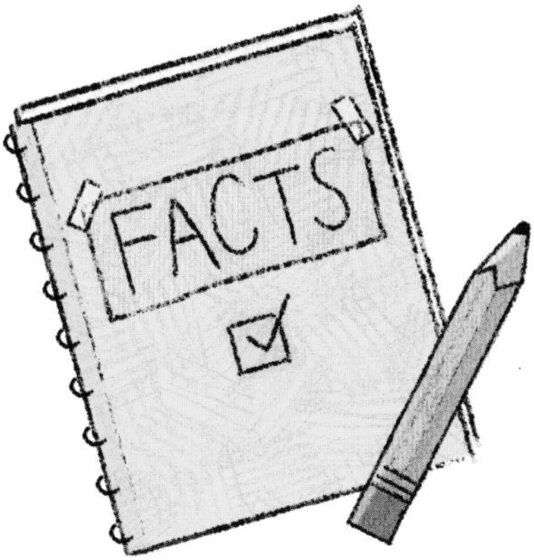
FACTS

For curious
Fact Collectors
everywhere

Chapter One

In the middle of the city is a strange street where the trees are all twisted. This is Evergreen Street.

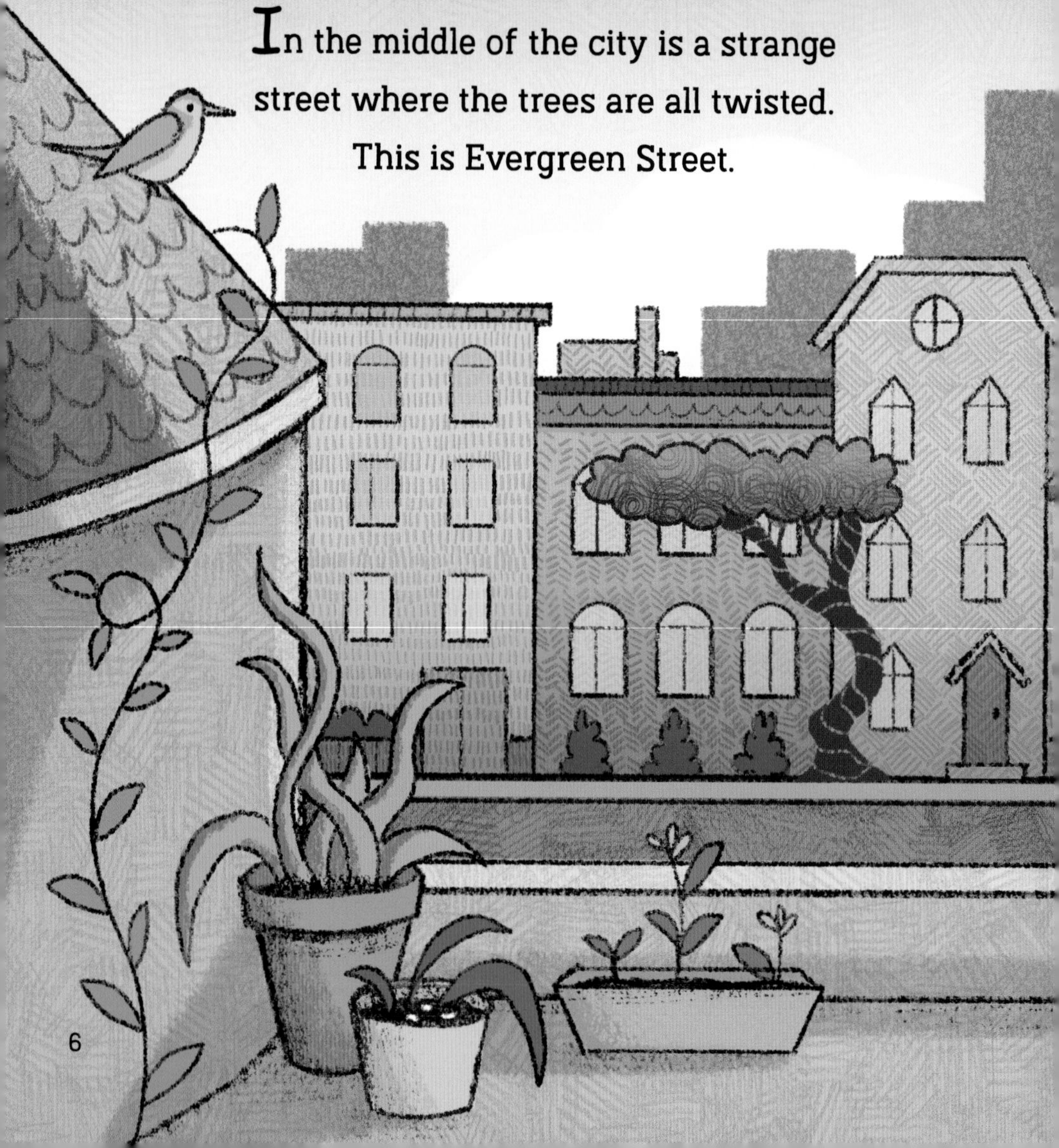

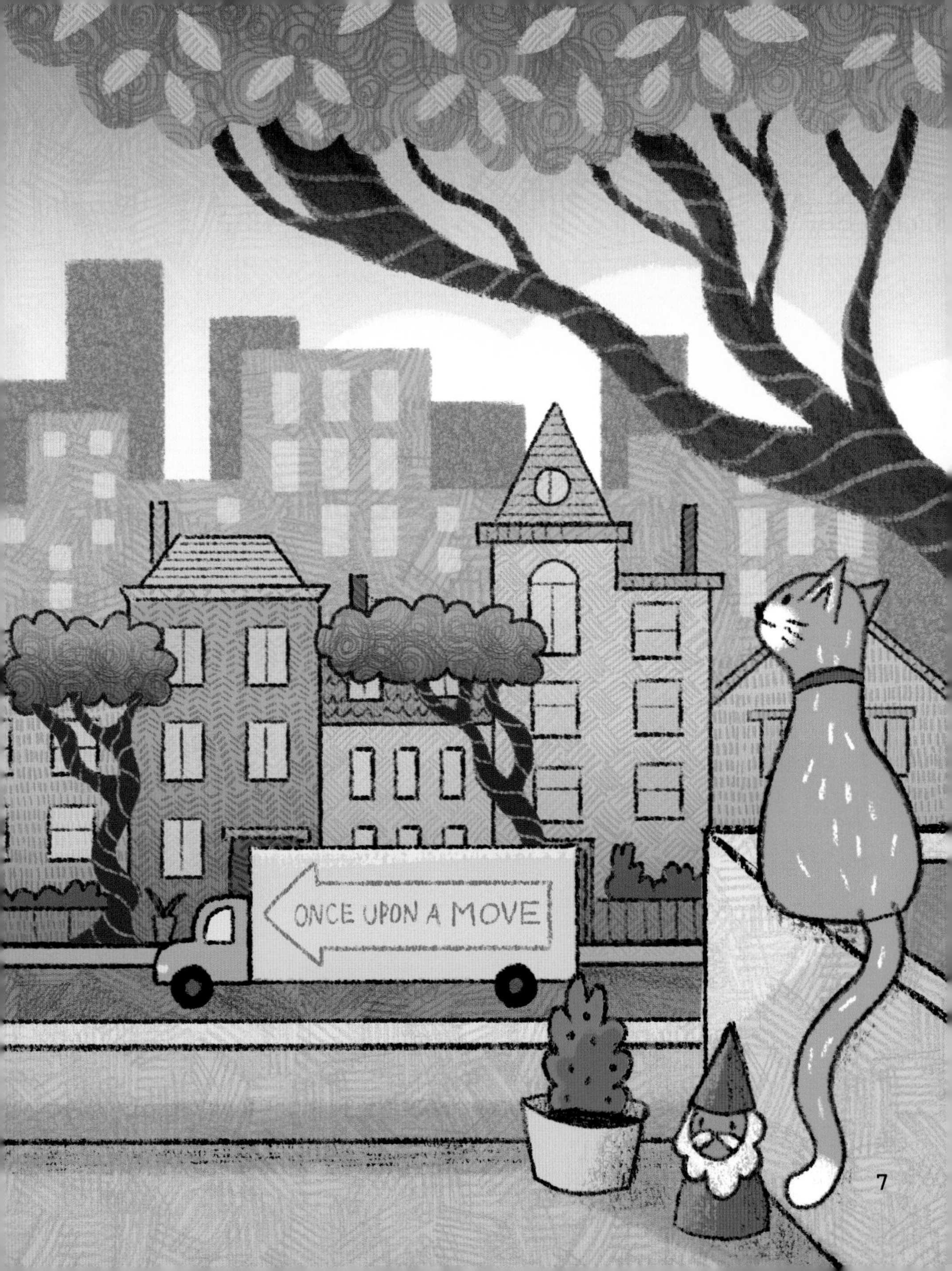
ONCE UPON A MOVE

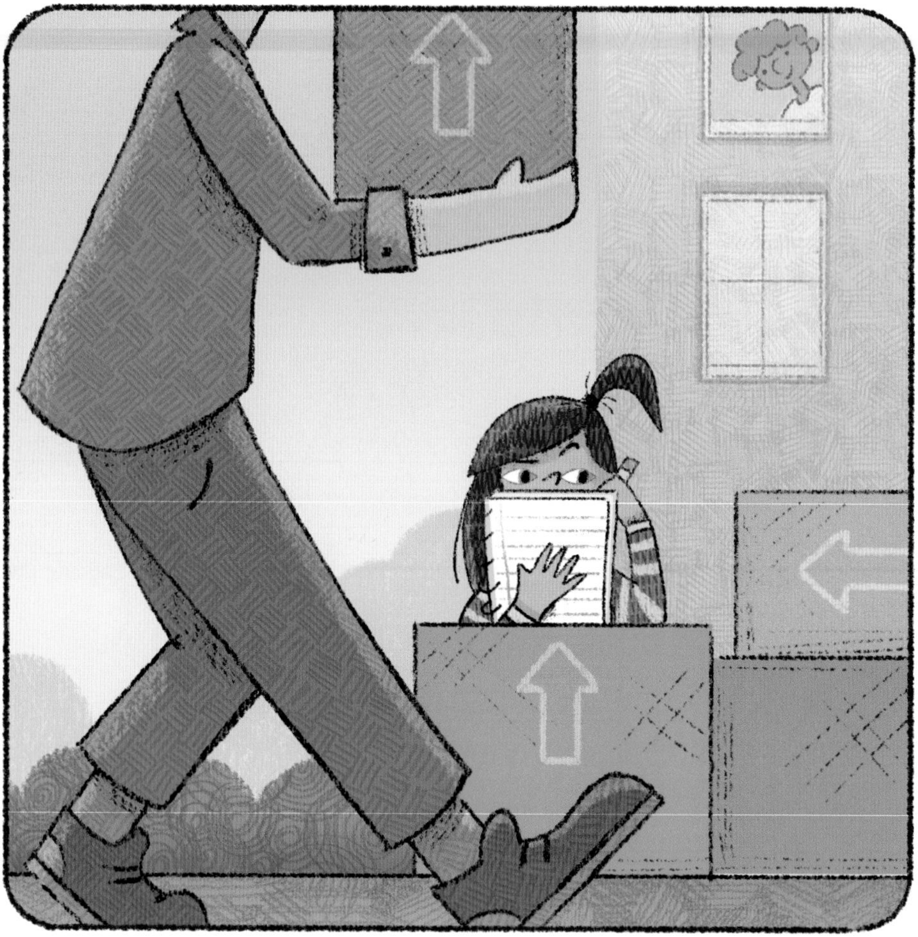

I am the newest resident of this street.

My name is Paige.

→ ALL ABOUT ME ←

Name: Paige Turner

Age: 8 years, 3 months, 14 days

favorite color
is yellow

collects facts
in Fact Diary

loves to read
nonfiction

always
double-knots
sneakers

Motto: If you can't prove it, it's not a fact!

I am a Fact Collector. A fact is a true piece of information. When I discover a fact I love, I write it in my Fact Diary.

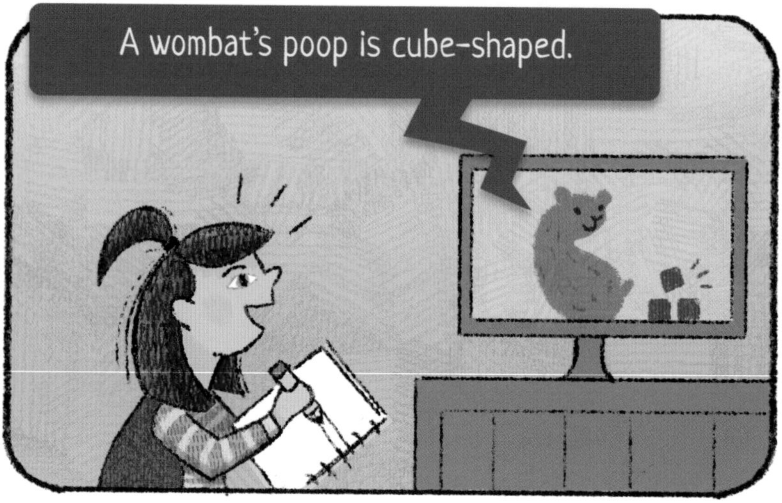
A wombat's poop is cube-shaped.

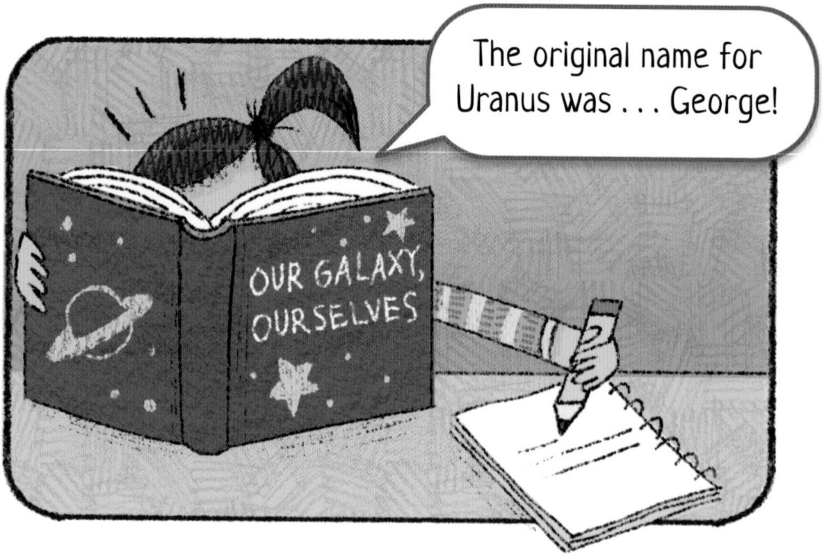
The original name for Uranus was . . . George!
OUR GALAXY, OURSELVES

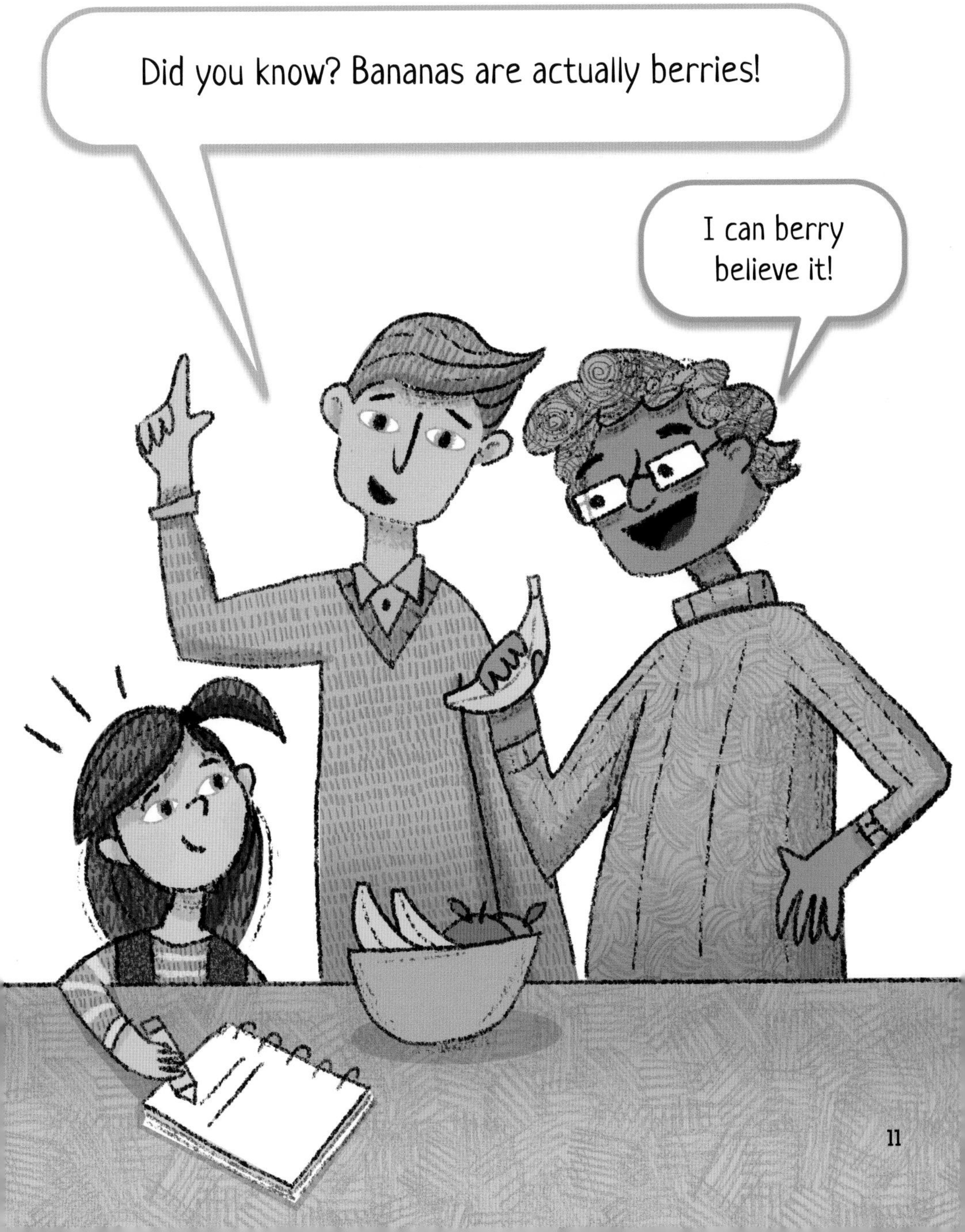
Did you know? Bananas are actually berries!
I can berry believe it!

When arriving in a new place, it is helpful to collect facts to feel at home. So far I have collected several facts about Evergreen Street.

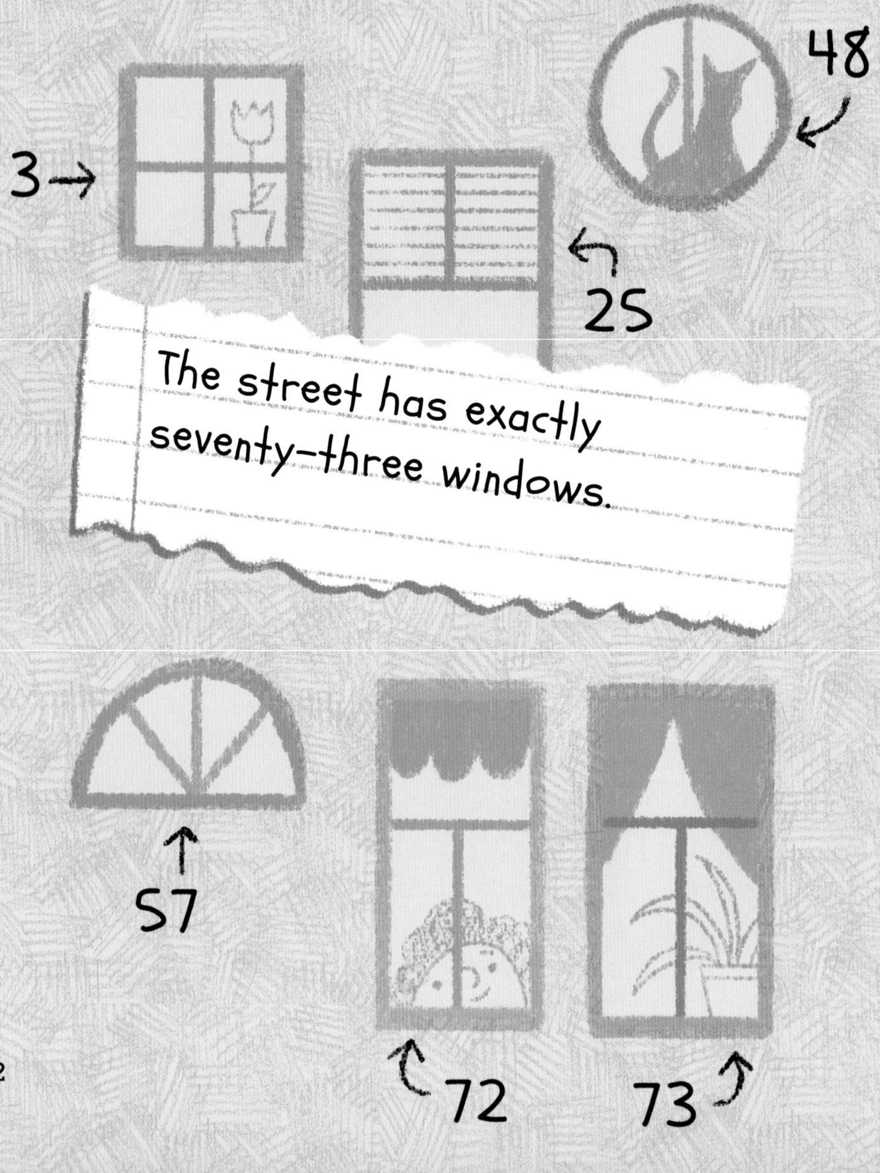
48
3
25
57
72
73

The street has exactly seventy-three windows.

Every full moon they have a street festival.

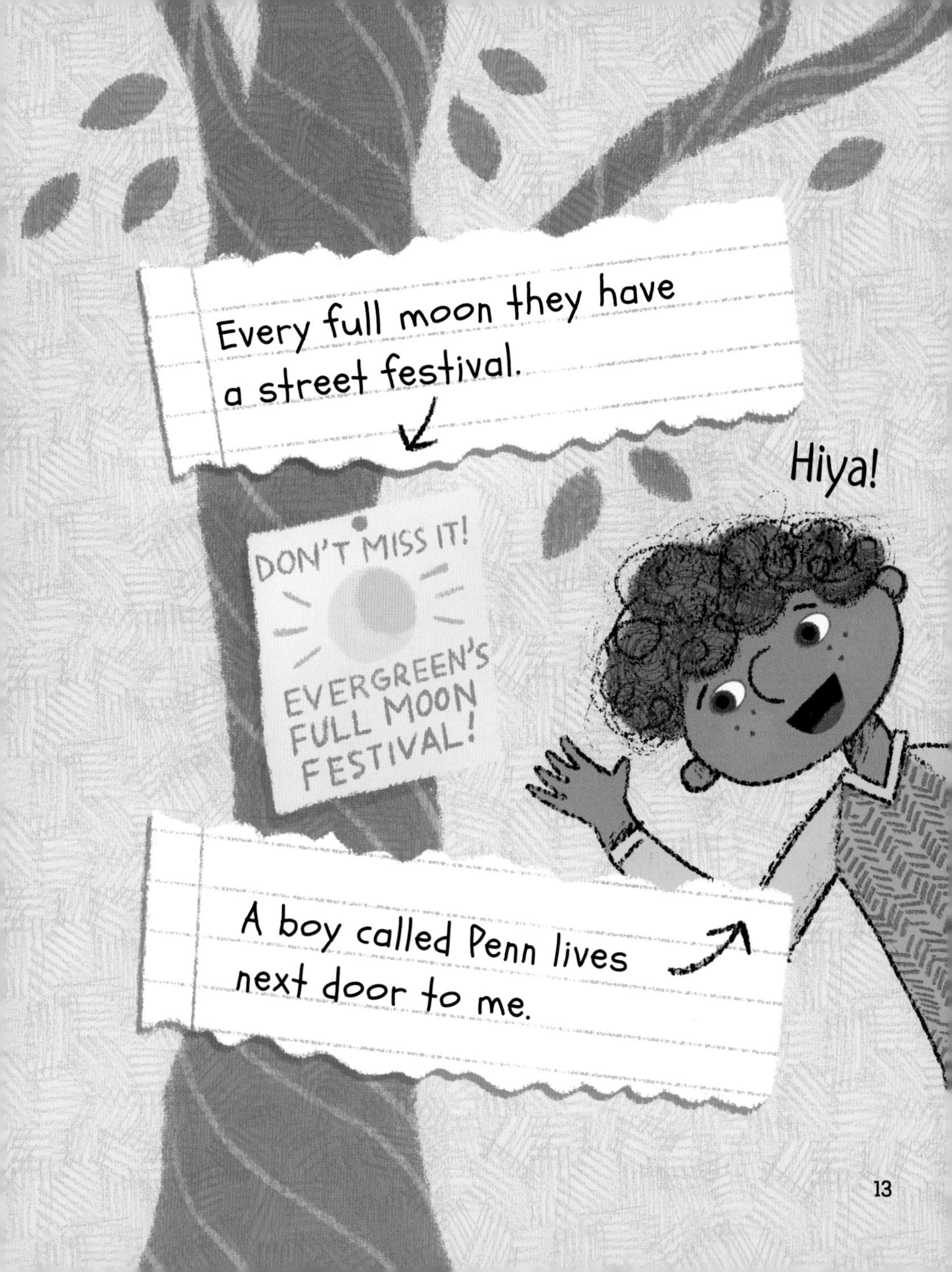
DON'T MISS IT!
EVERGREEN'S FULL MOON FESTIVAL!
Hiya!

A boy called Penn lives next door to me.

Name: Penn

Age: 6 months in cat years
(8 human years)

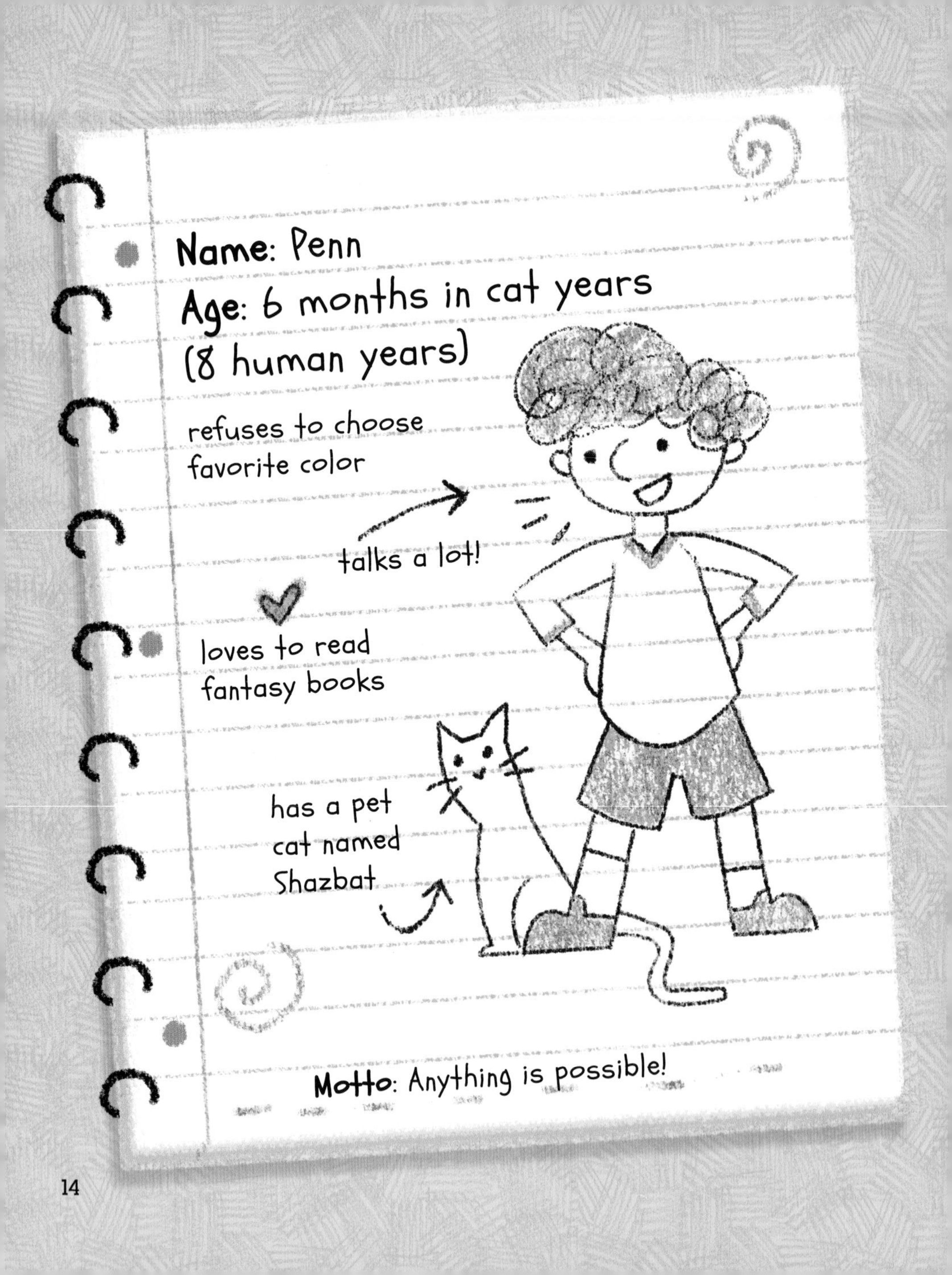

refuses to choose
favorite color

talks a lot!

loves to read
fantasy books

has a pet
cat named
Shazbat

Motto: Anything is possible!

Penn loves to talk almost as much
as I love to collect facts!

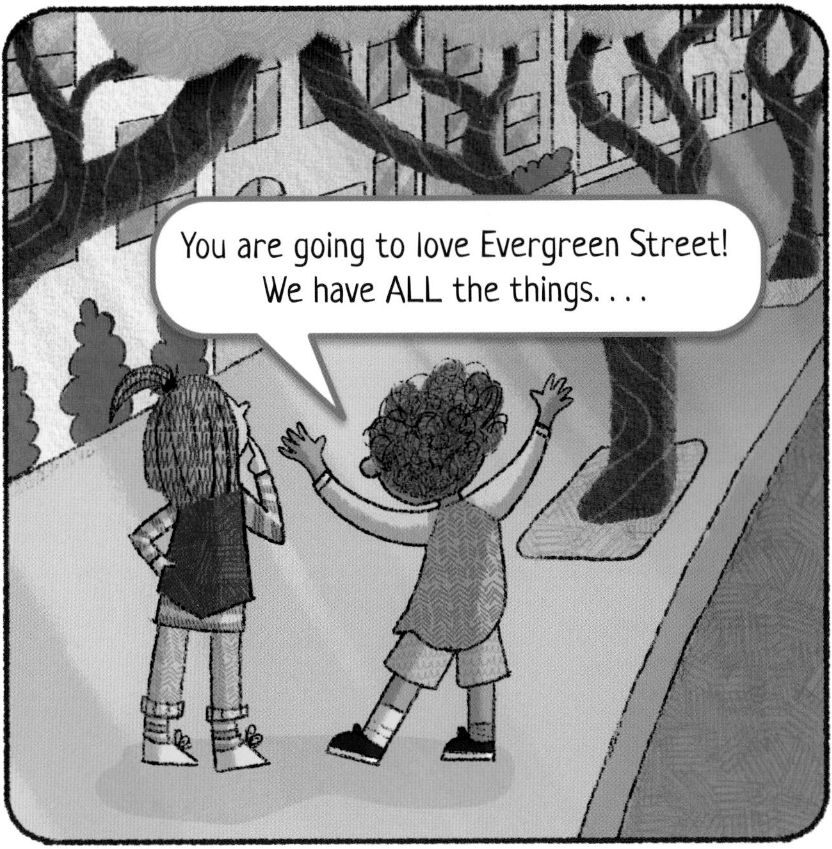
You are going to love Evergreen Street! We have ALL the things. . . .

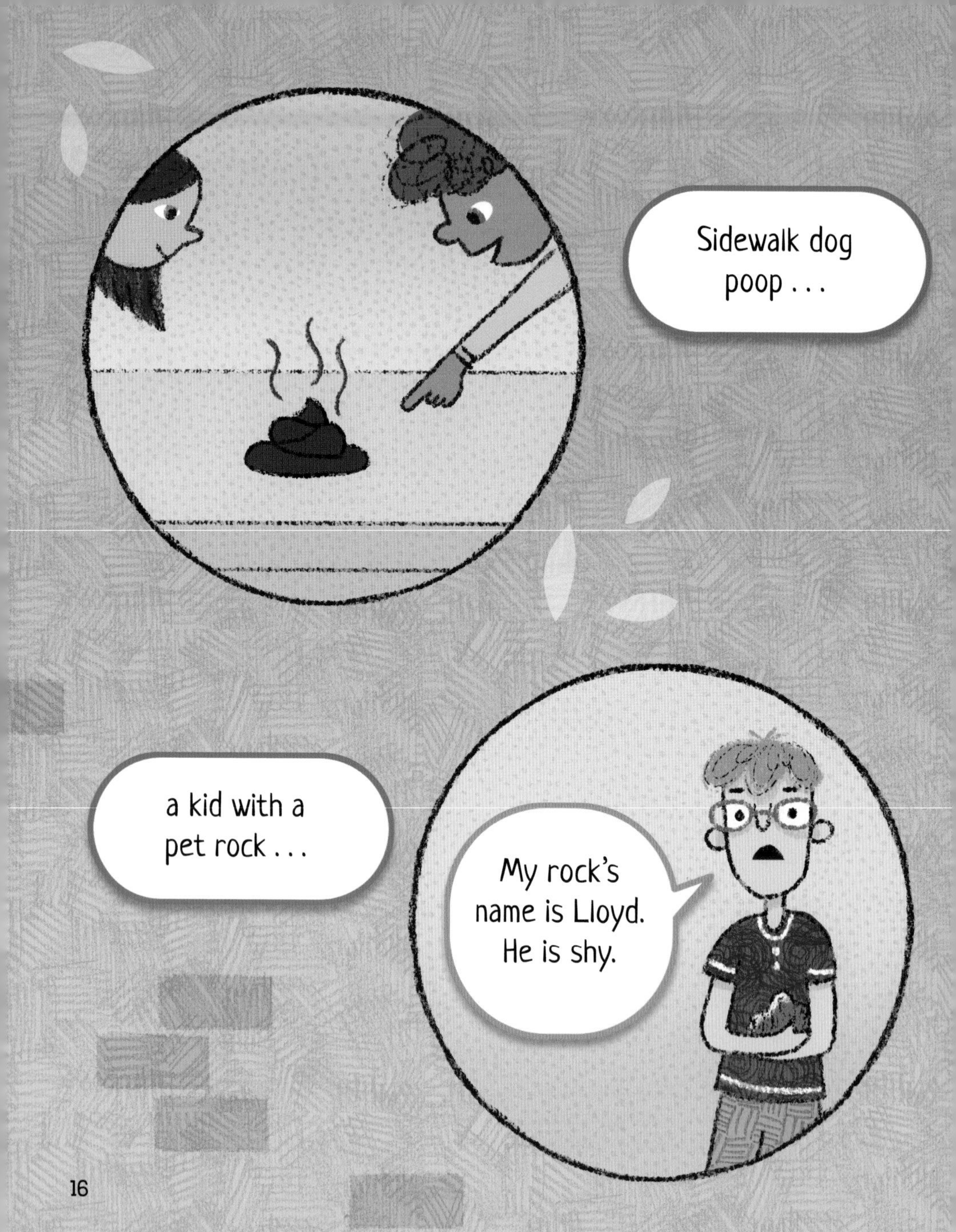

Sidewalk dog poop . . .
a kid with a pet rock . . .
My rock's name is Lloyd. He is shy.

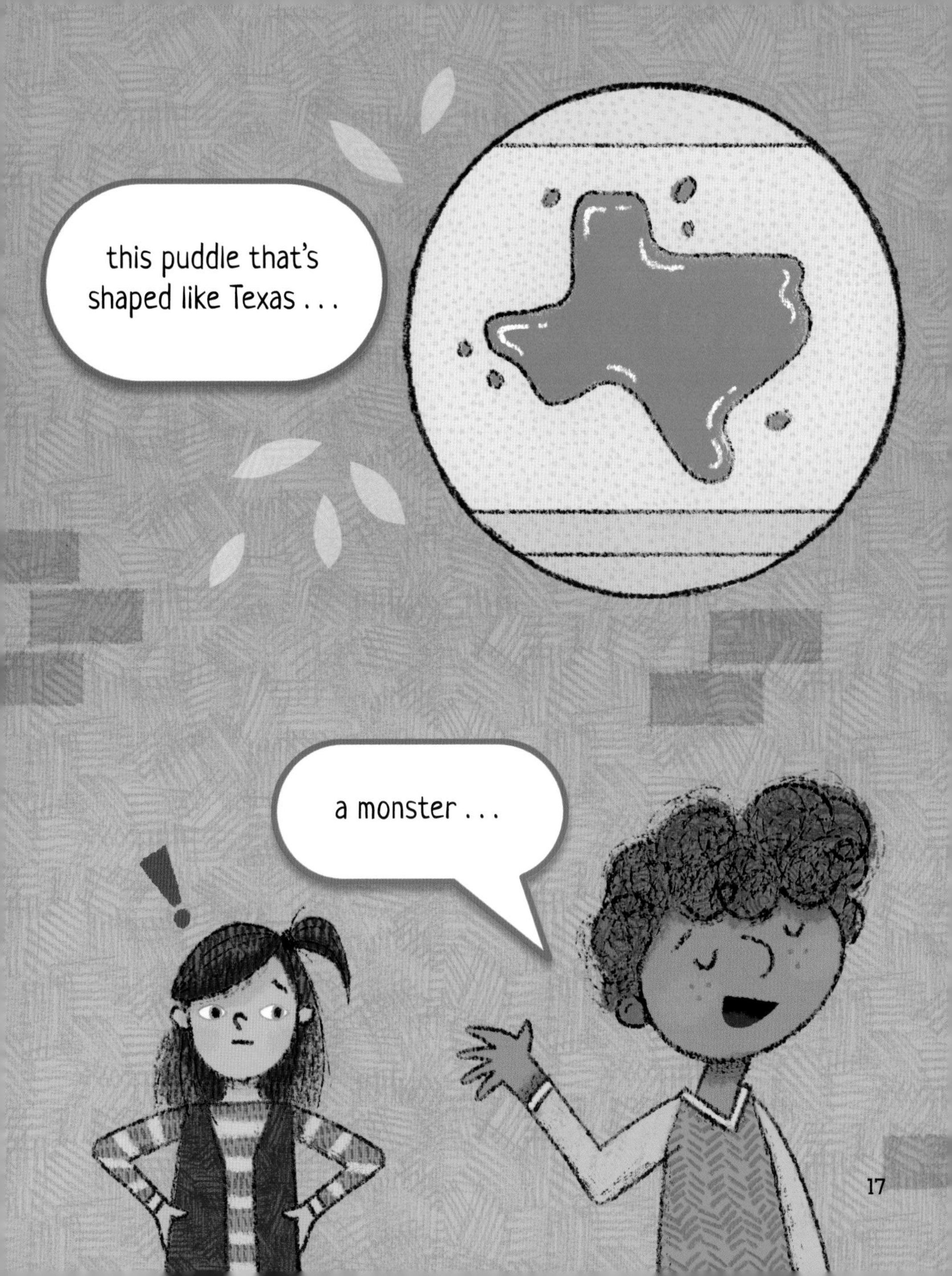
this puddle that's shaped like Texas . . .
a monster . . .

STOP!

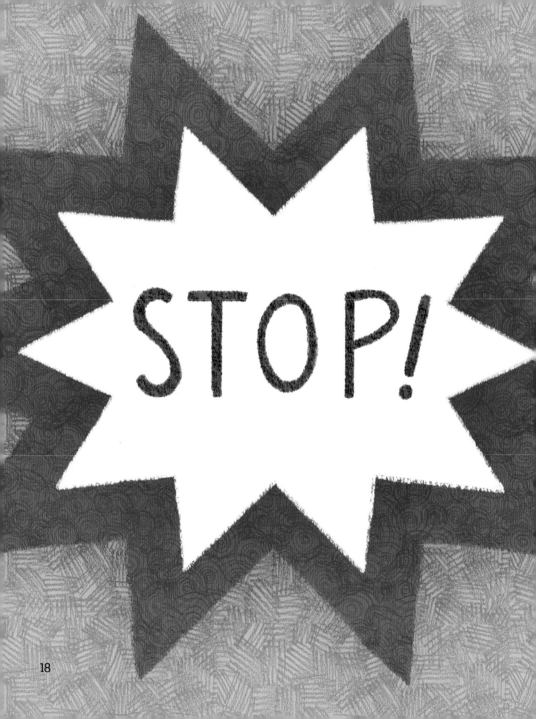

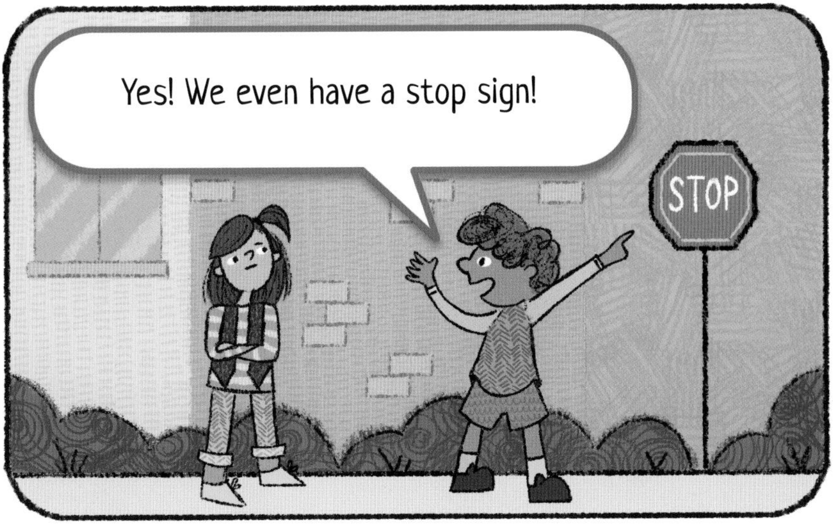
Yes! We even have a stop sign!
STOP

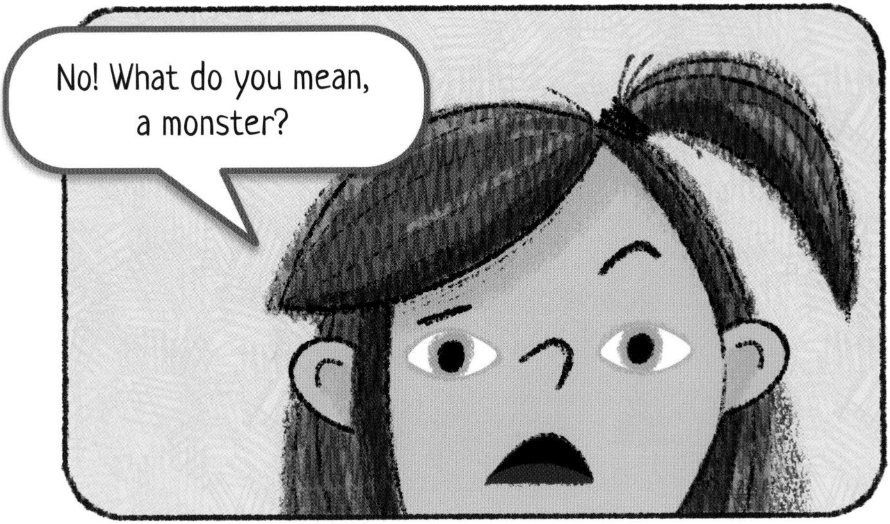
No! What do you mean,
a monster?

Chapter Two

I stopped in my tracks.
Did he just say what
I thought he said?

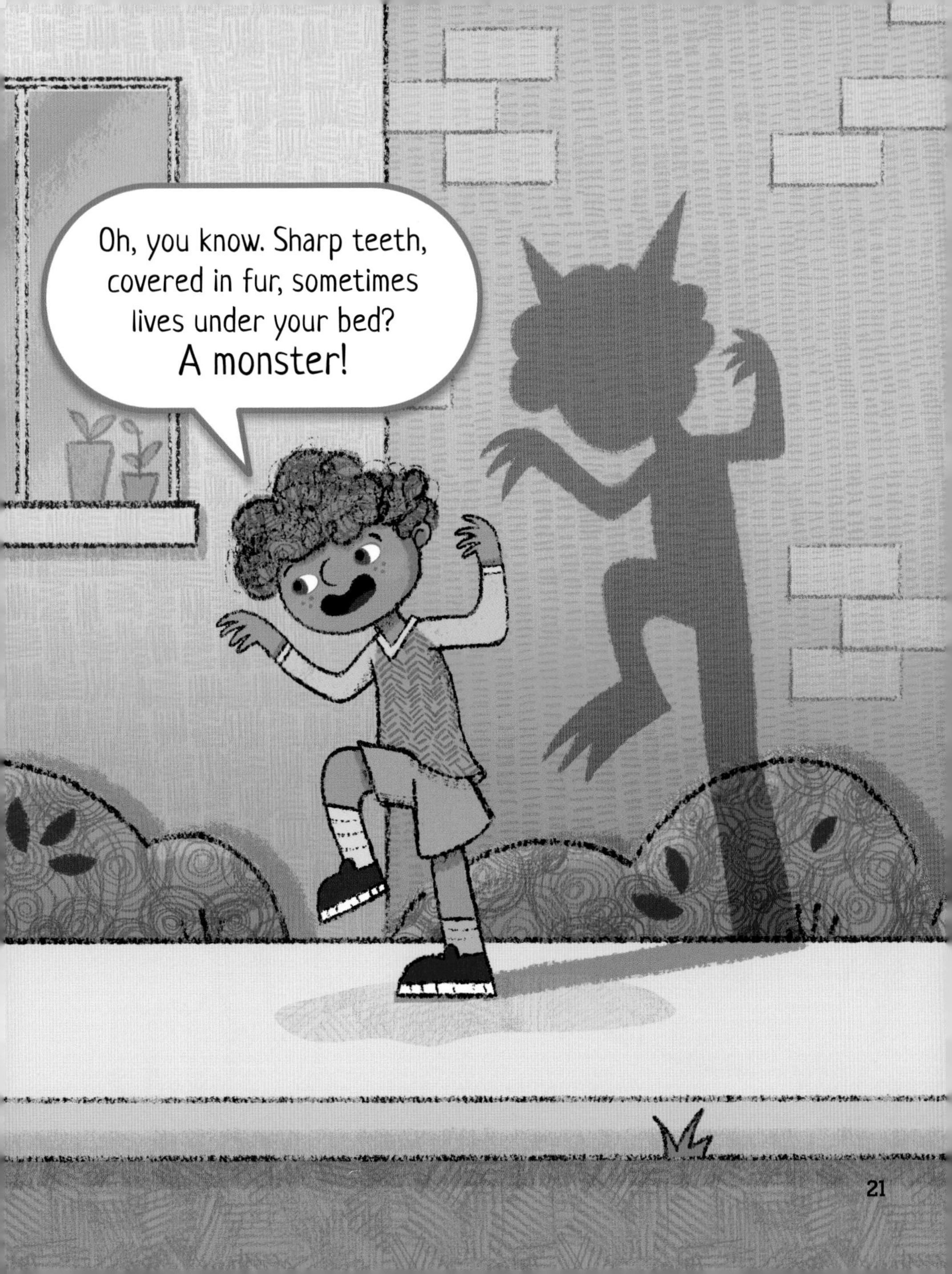
Oh, you know. Sharp teeth, covered in fur, sometimes lives under your bed? A monster!

As a Fact Collector, it is my responsibility to tell people when they are wrong.

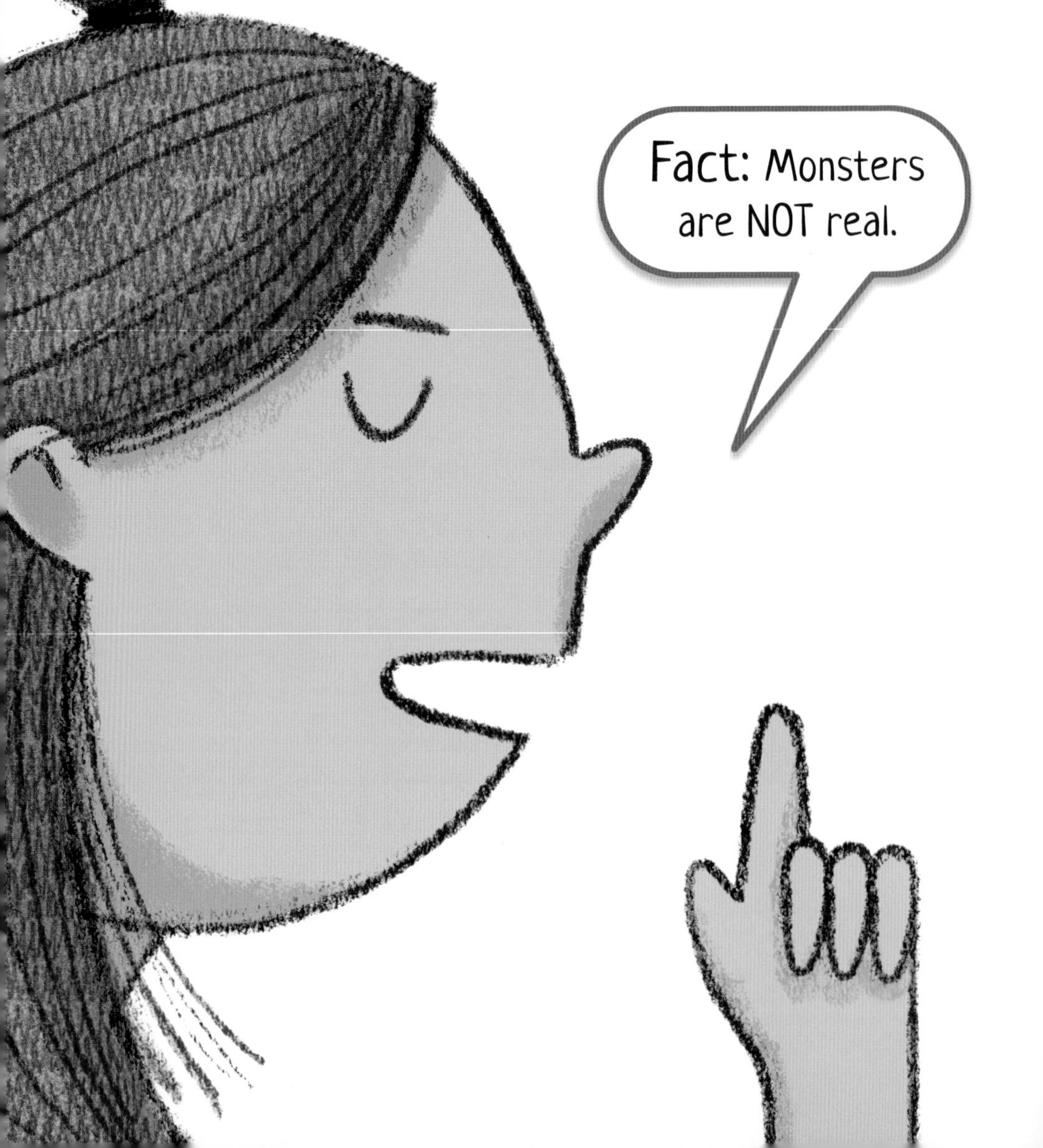
Fact: Monsters are NOT real.

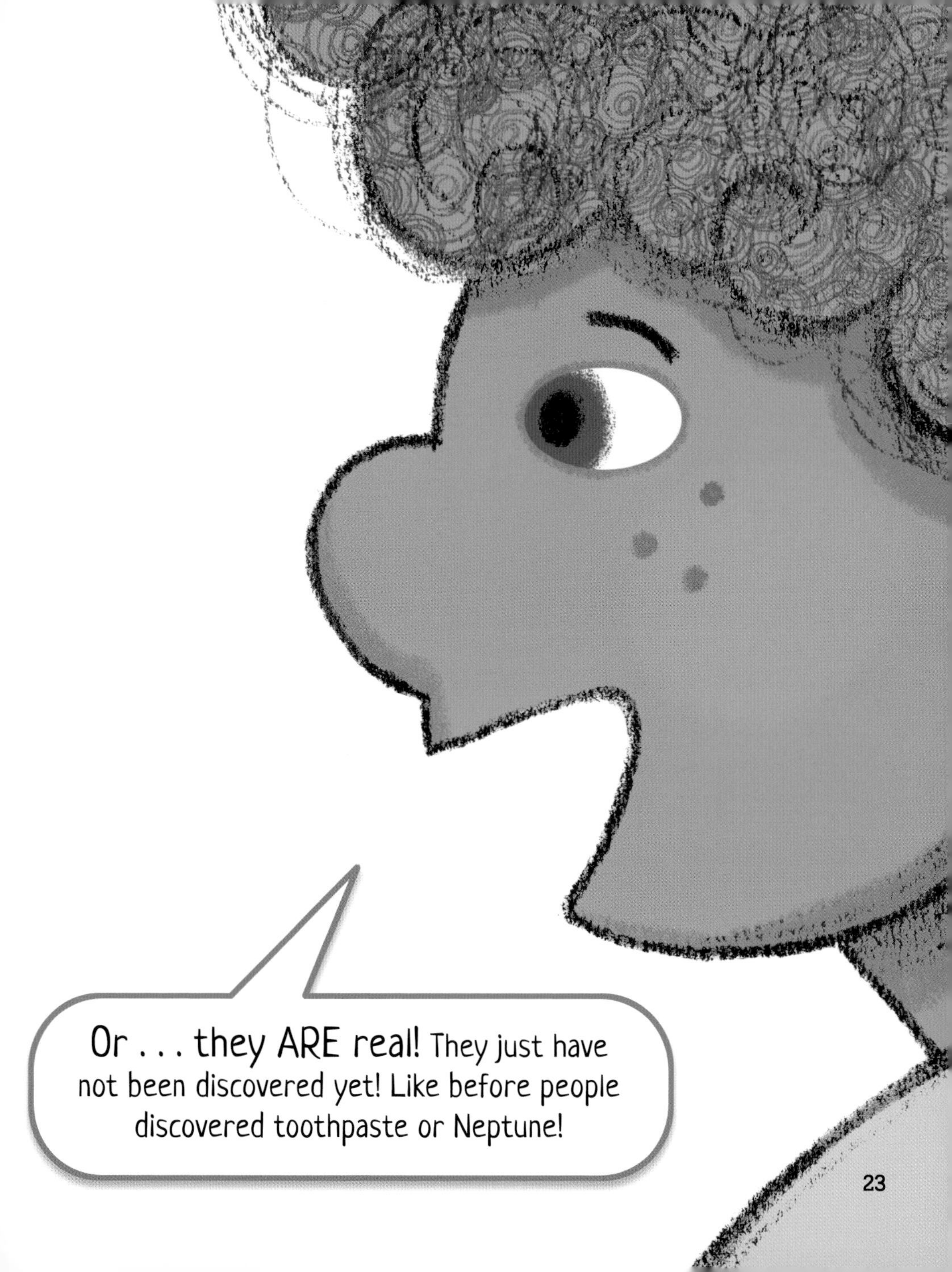
Or . . . they ARE real! They just have not been discovered yet! Like before people discovered toothpaste or Neptune!

It's hard to admit, but Penn makes a good point.

Fact: Neptune is a planet that was discovered in 1846.

Found you!

But before that, some very smart people only **GUESSED** that it was there.

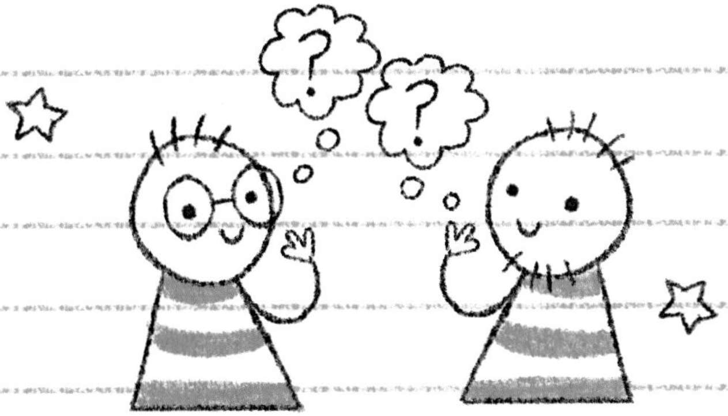
?
?

They had to do a lot of tricky math to **PROVE** their guess was, in fact . . . **A FACT!**

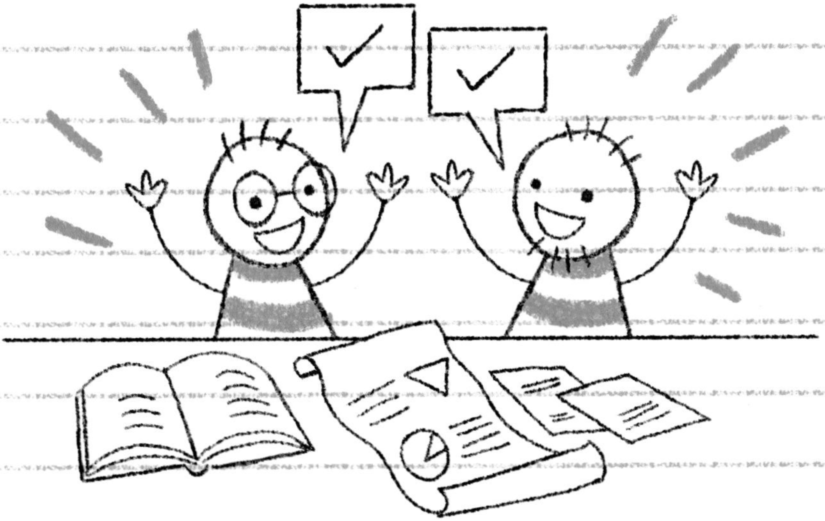

All facts start off as guesses.

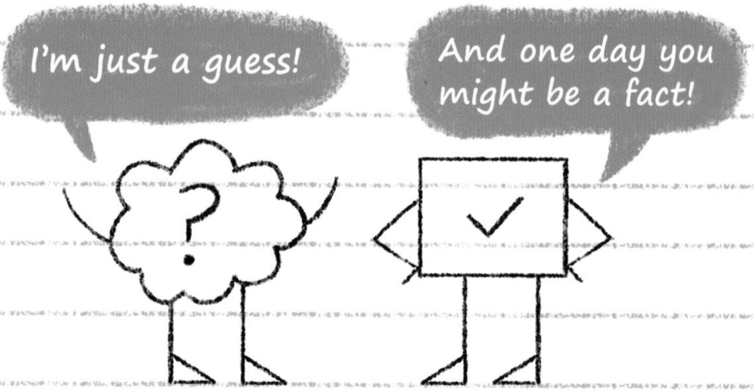
I'm just a guess!
And one day you might be a fact!

But with evidence, a guess can be proven to be a fact . . . or not.

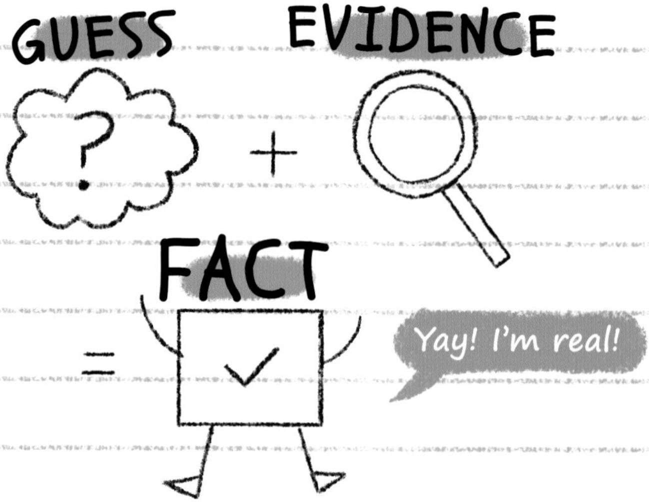
GUESS
EVIDENCE
FACT
Yay! I'm real!

As Penn is telling me about the undiscovered monster of Evergreen Street . . . I have an idea!

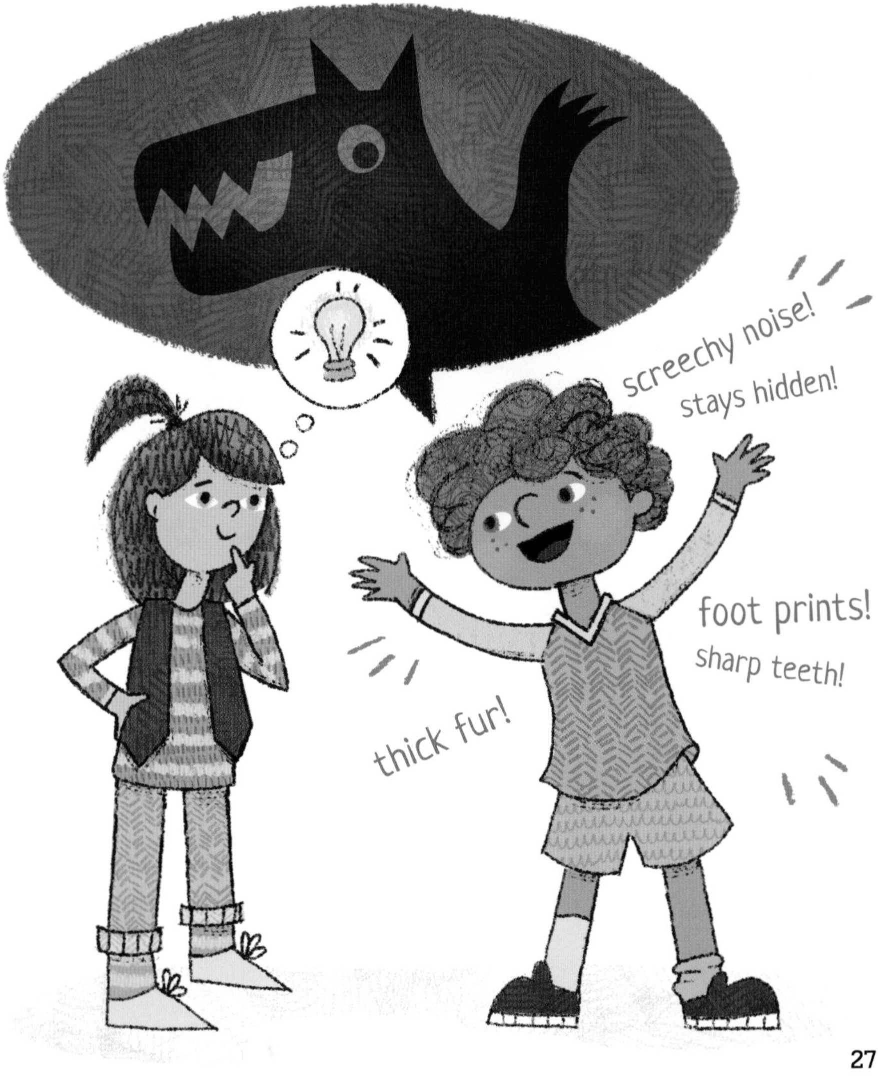
screechy noise!
stays hidden!
foot prints!
sharp teeth!
thick fur!

What if I, Paige the Fact Collector, could prove whether the guess about this monster, was a fact? Then I could write a fact in my Fact Diary, a fact that I had proven myself!

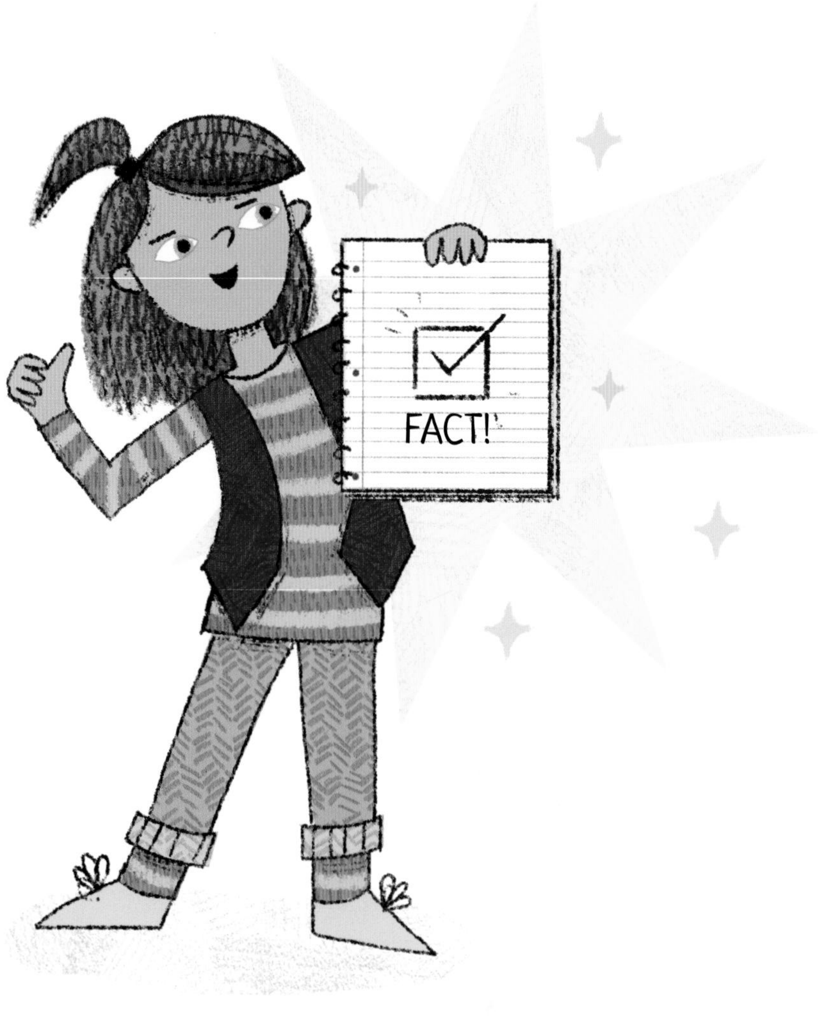
FACT!

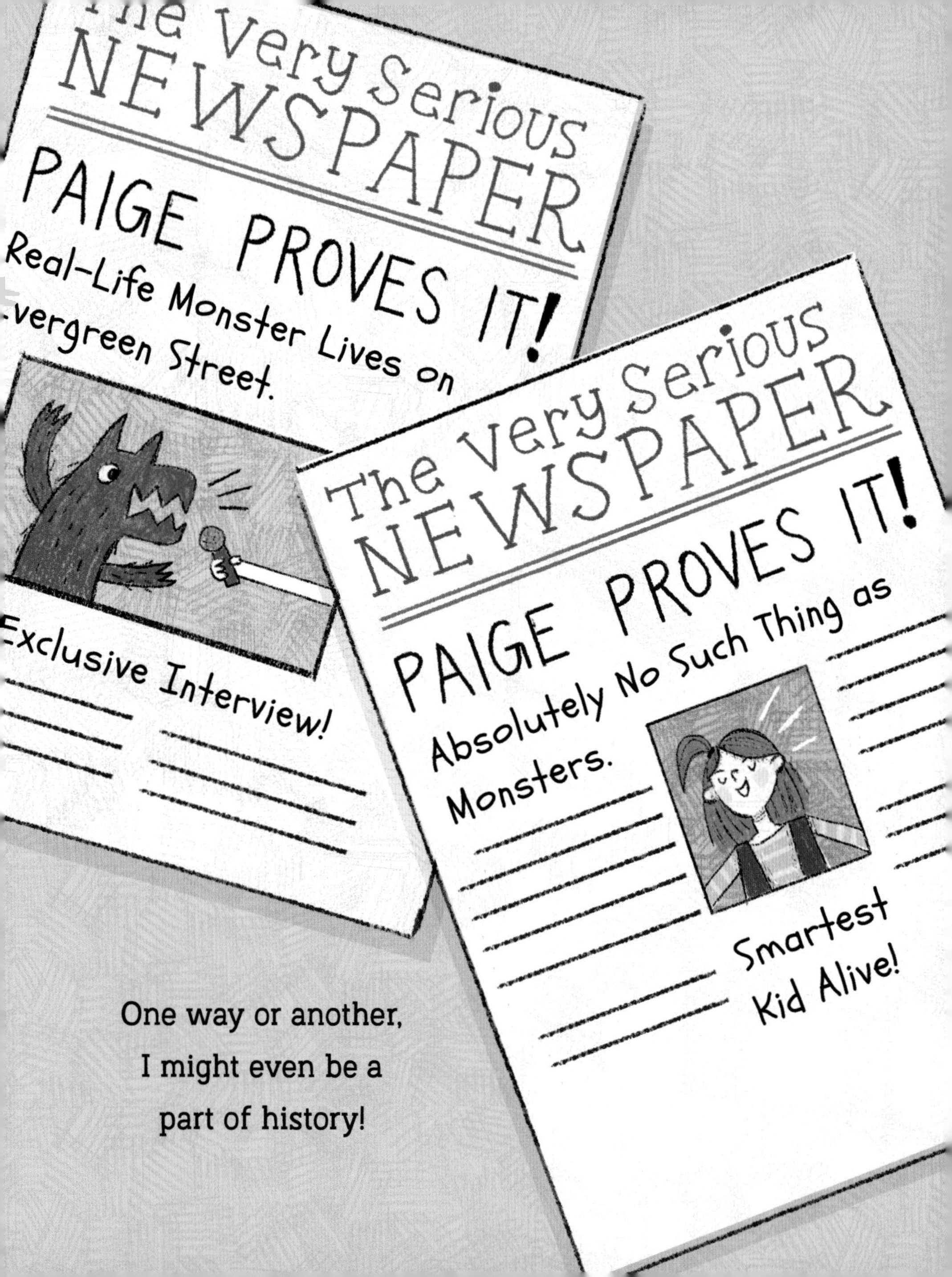
he Very Serious
NEWSPAPER
PAIGE PROVES IT!
Real-Life Monster Lives on
vergreen Street.
Exclusive Interview!
The Very Serious
NEWSPAPER
PAIGE PROVES IT!
Absolutely No Such Thing as
Monsters.
Smartest
Kid Alive!

One way or another,
I might even be a
part of history!

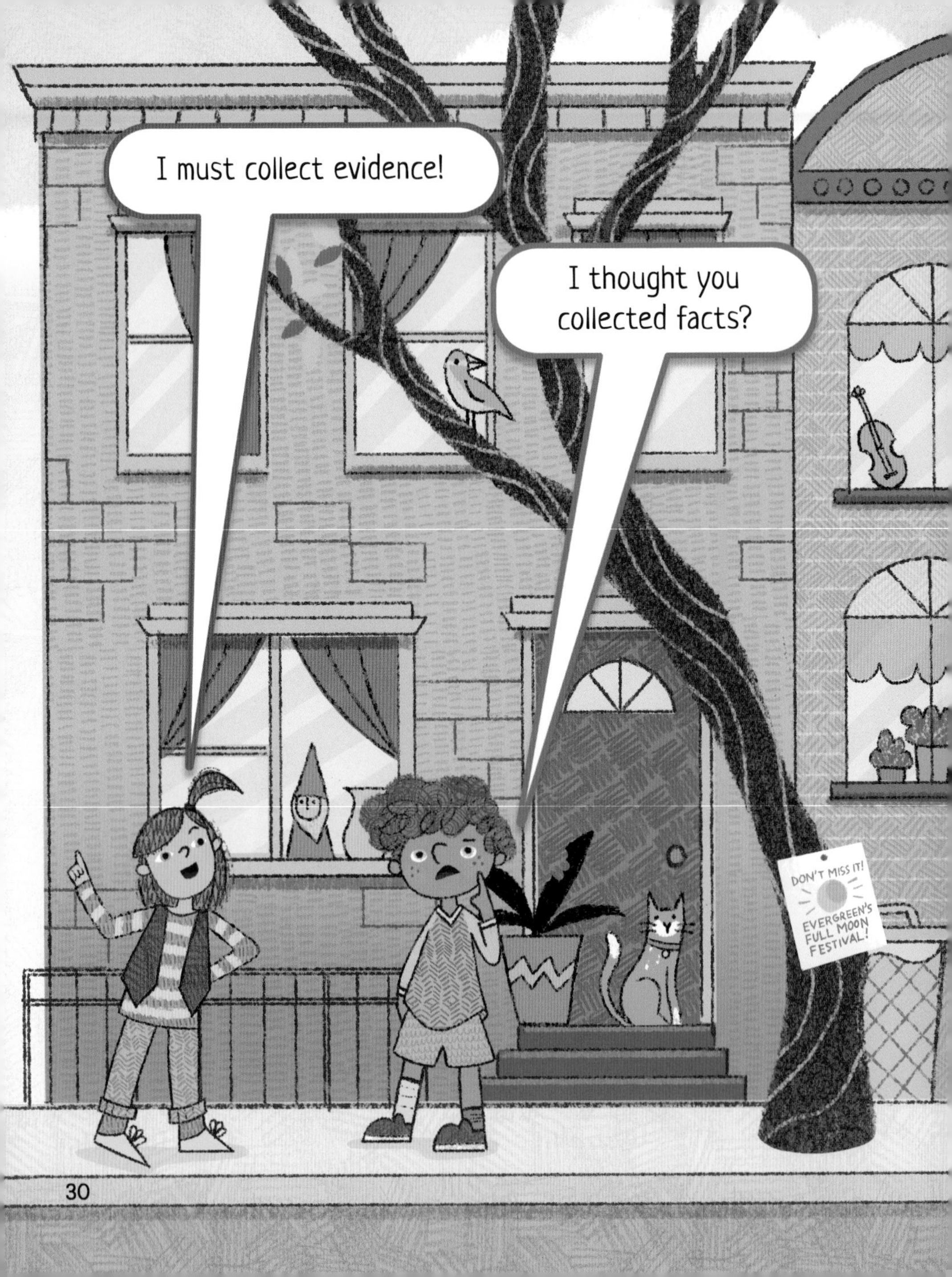
I must collect evidence!
I thought you collected facts?
DON'T MISS IT!
EVERGREEN'S FULL MOON FESTIVAL!

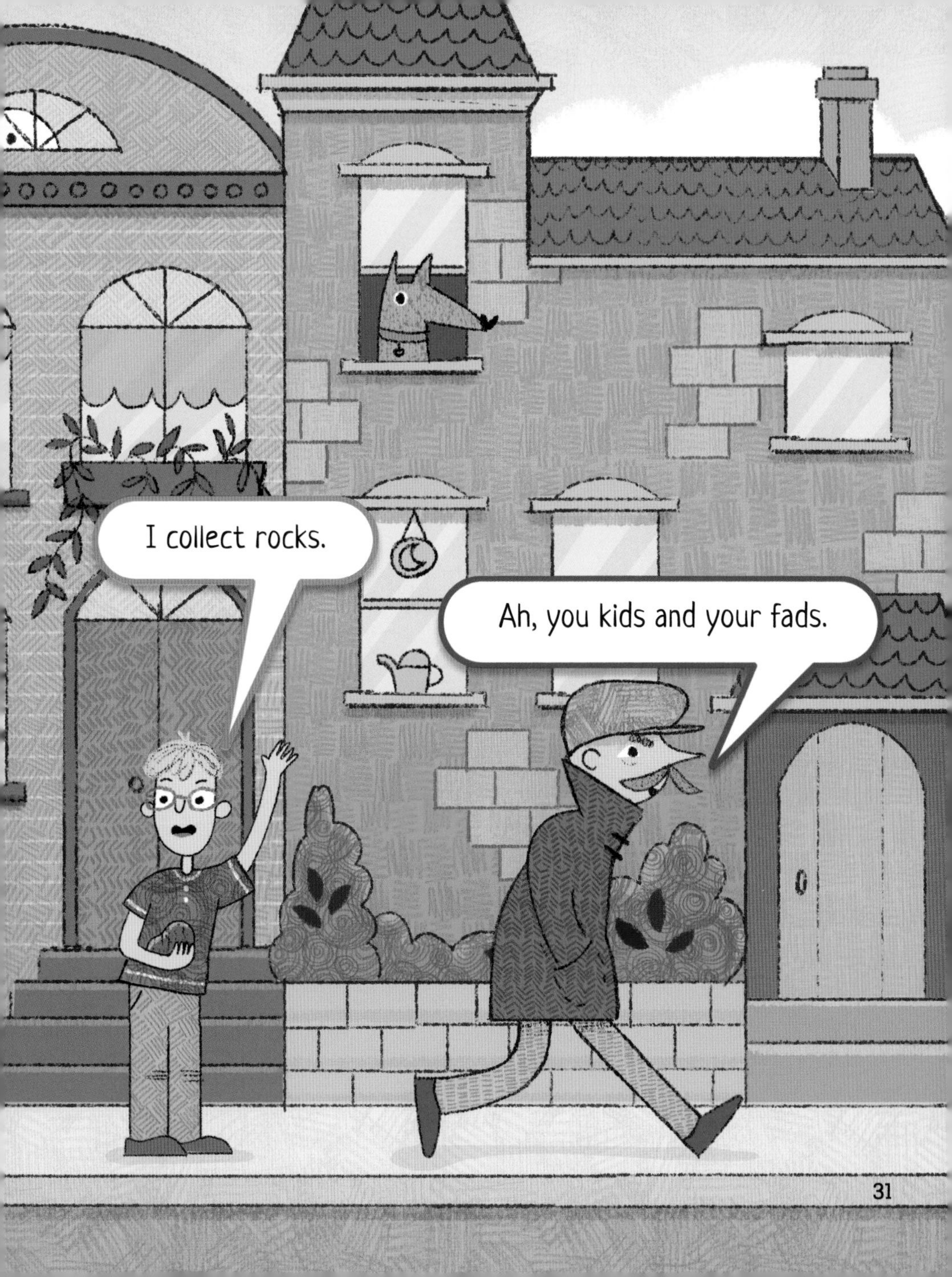
I collect rocks.
Ah, you kids and your fads.

Chapter Three

We need evidence to prove whether the monster is a fact, and evidence needs to be INVESTIGATED. With Penn's help, I make a list.

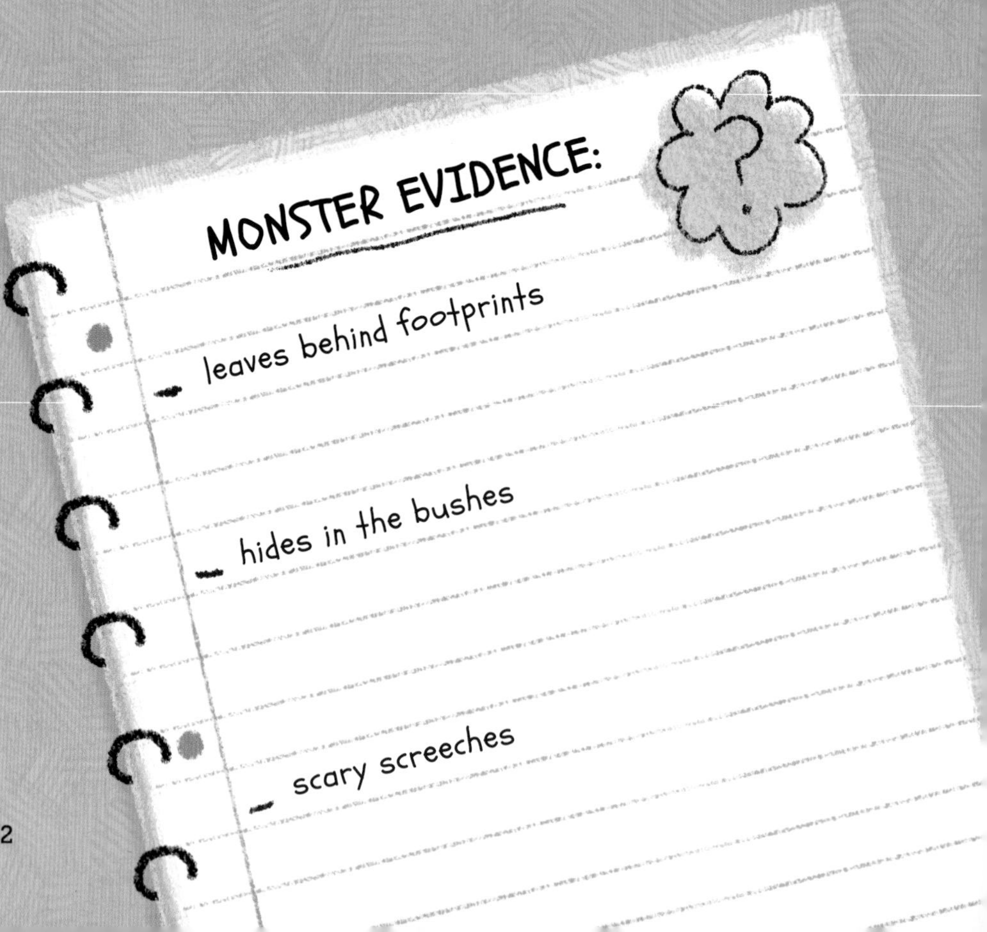
MONSTER EVIDENCE:
?
- leaves behind footprints
- hides in the bushes
- scary screeches

That means I need to see these monster-size footprints for myself.

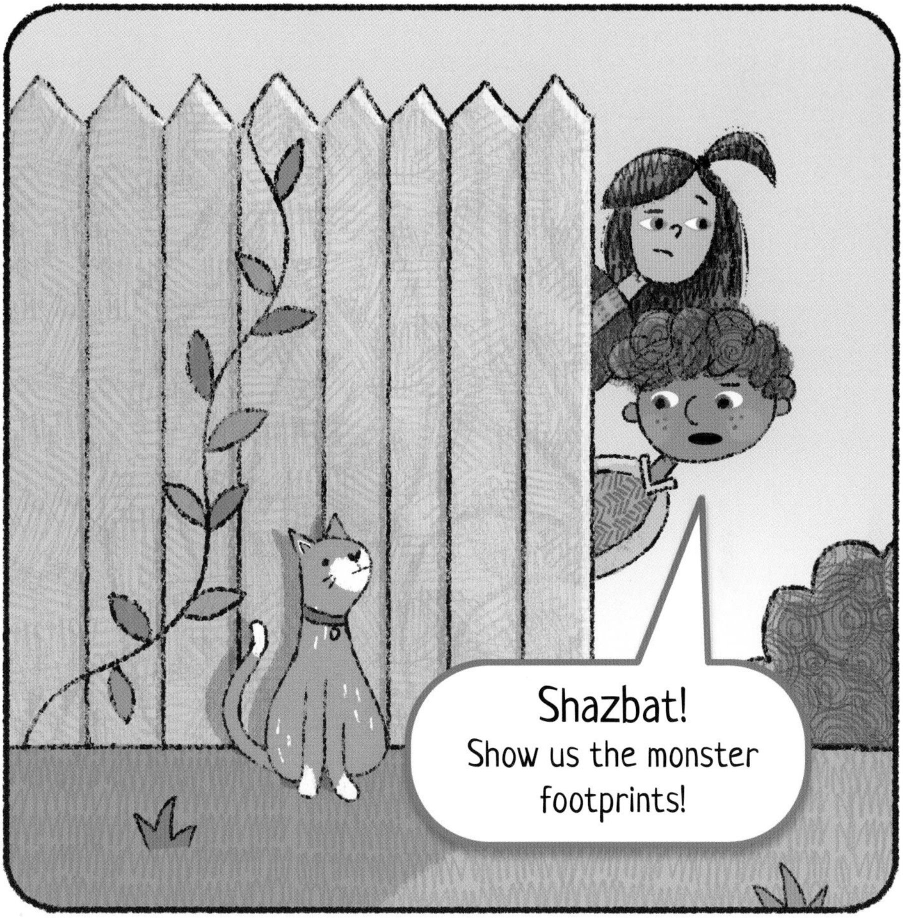
Shazbat!
Show us the monster footprints!

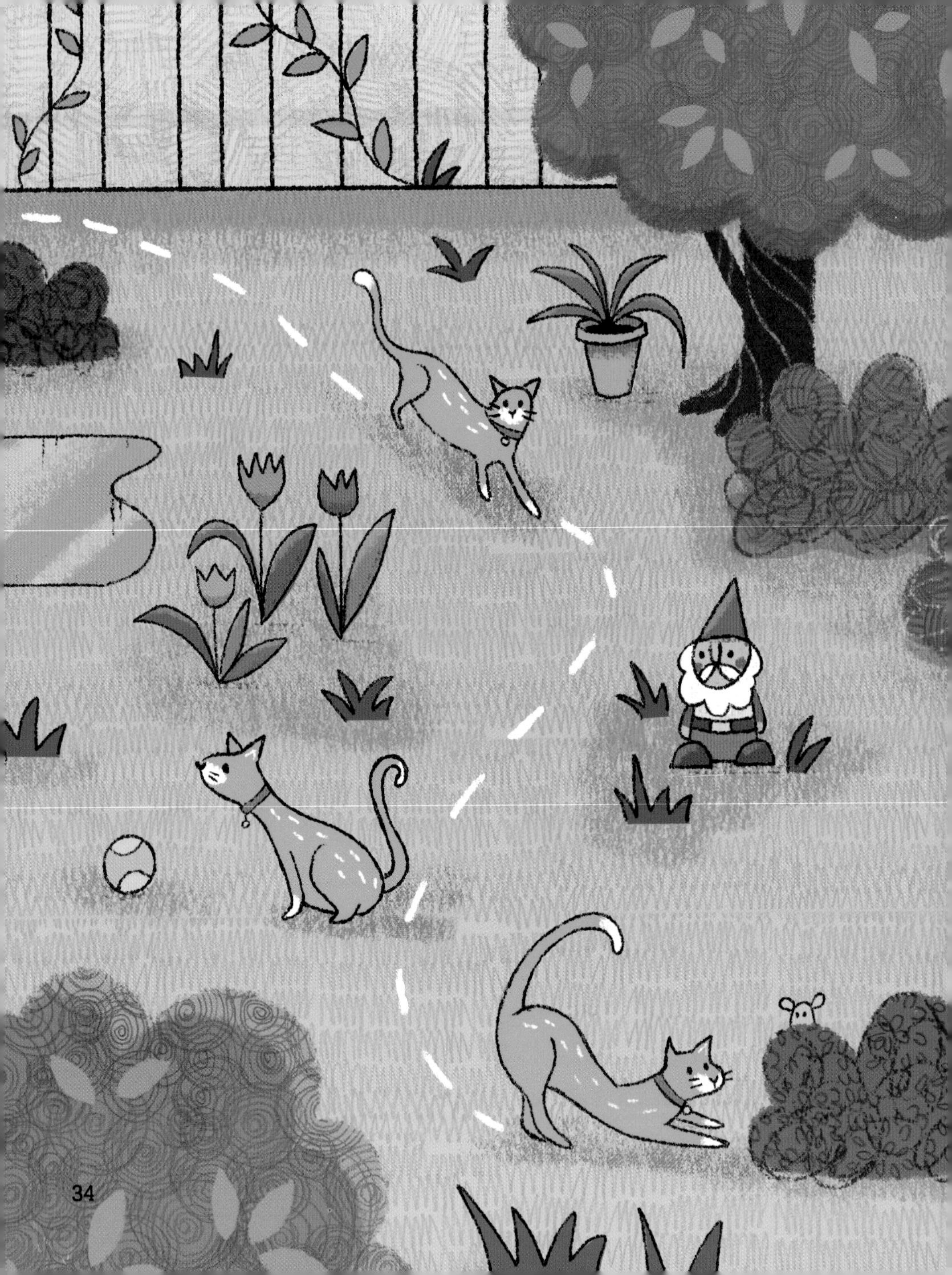

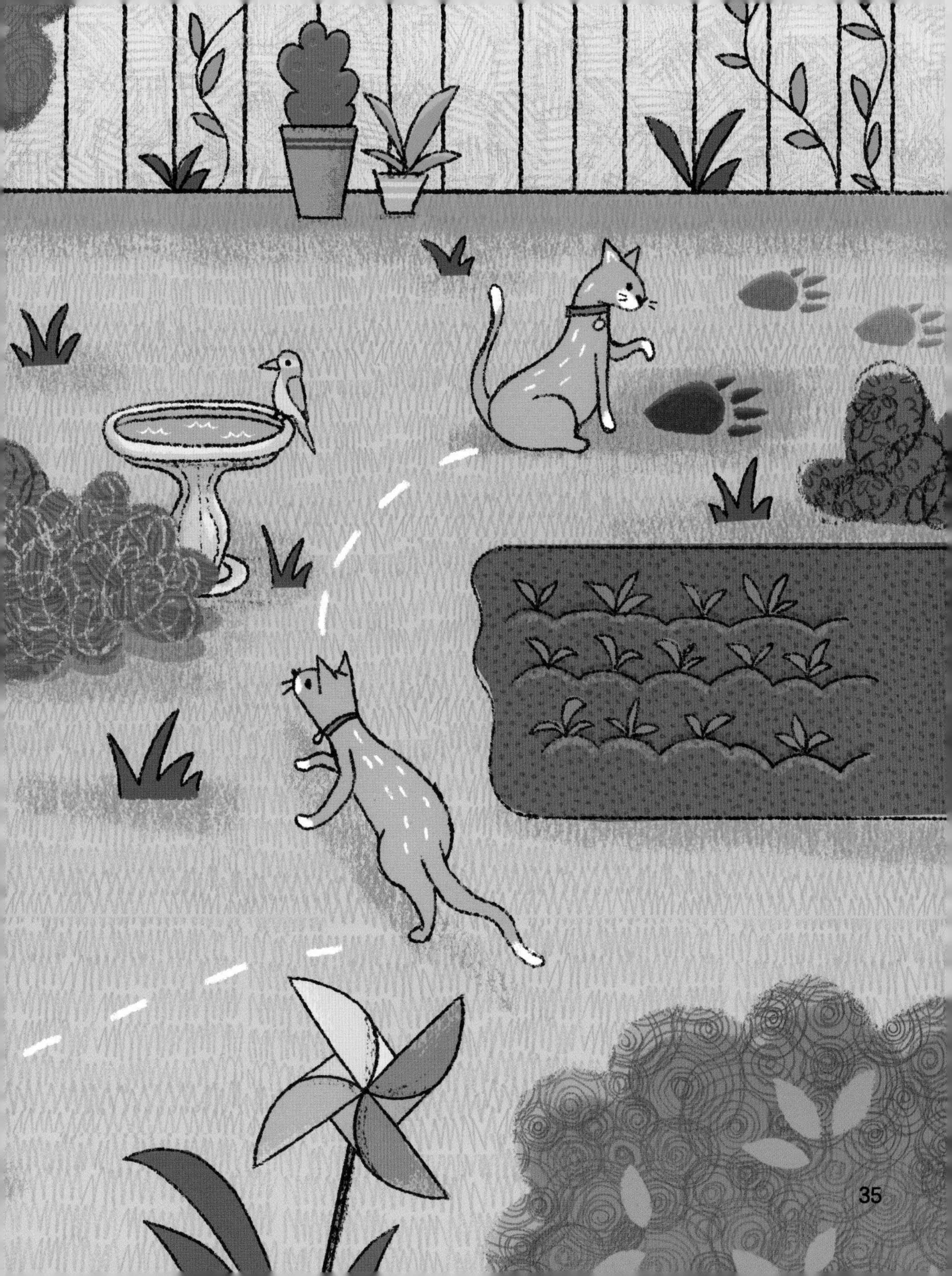

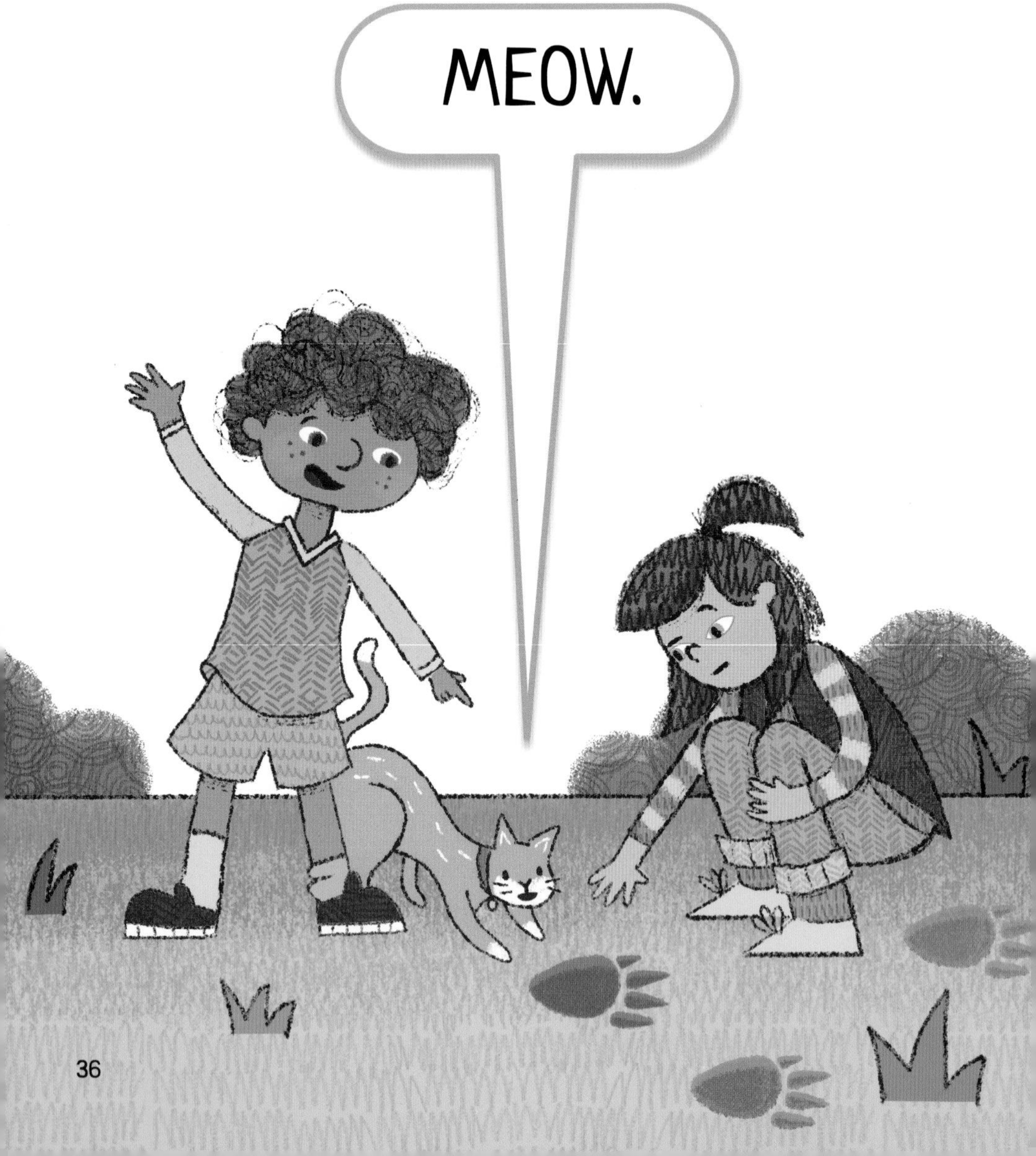
MEOW.

They are curious footprints.
I do my best to capture the size
and shape in my notebook.

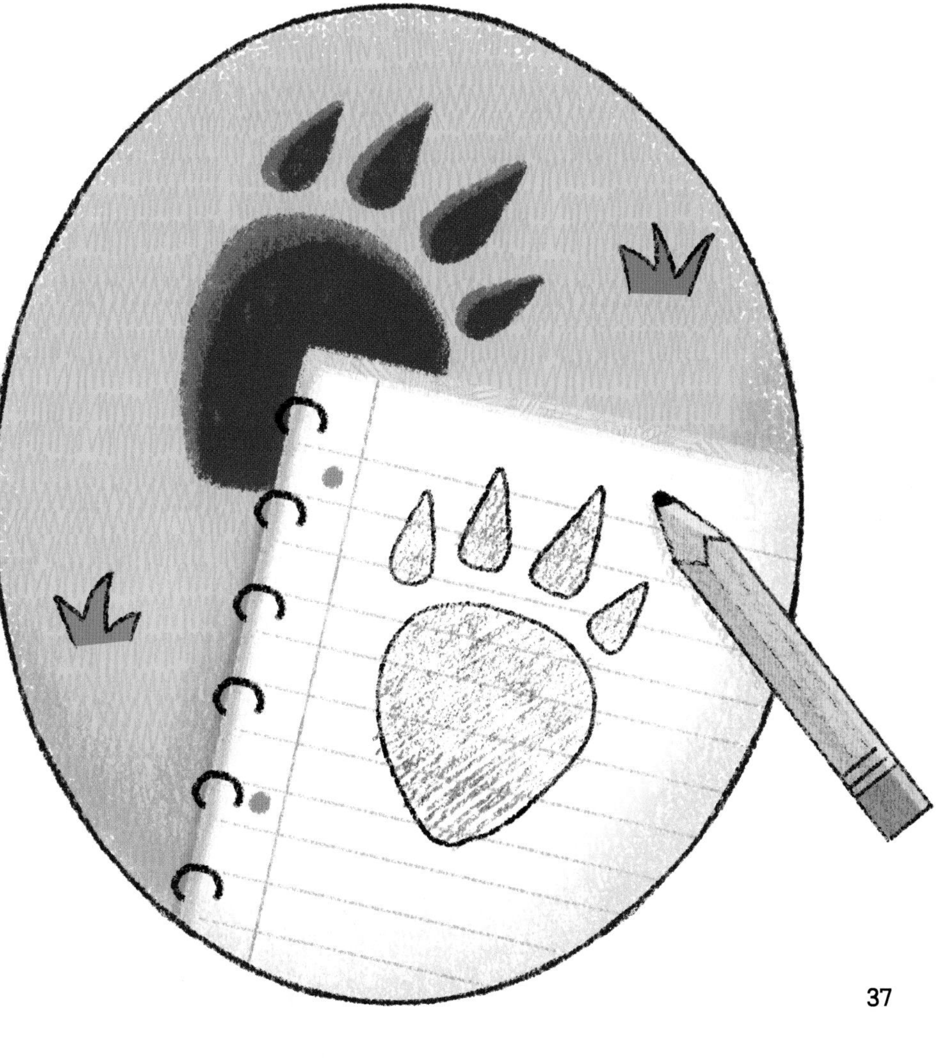

But does this footprint really
belong to a monster?

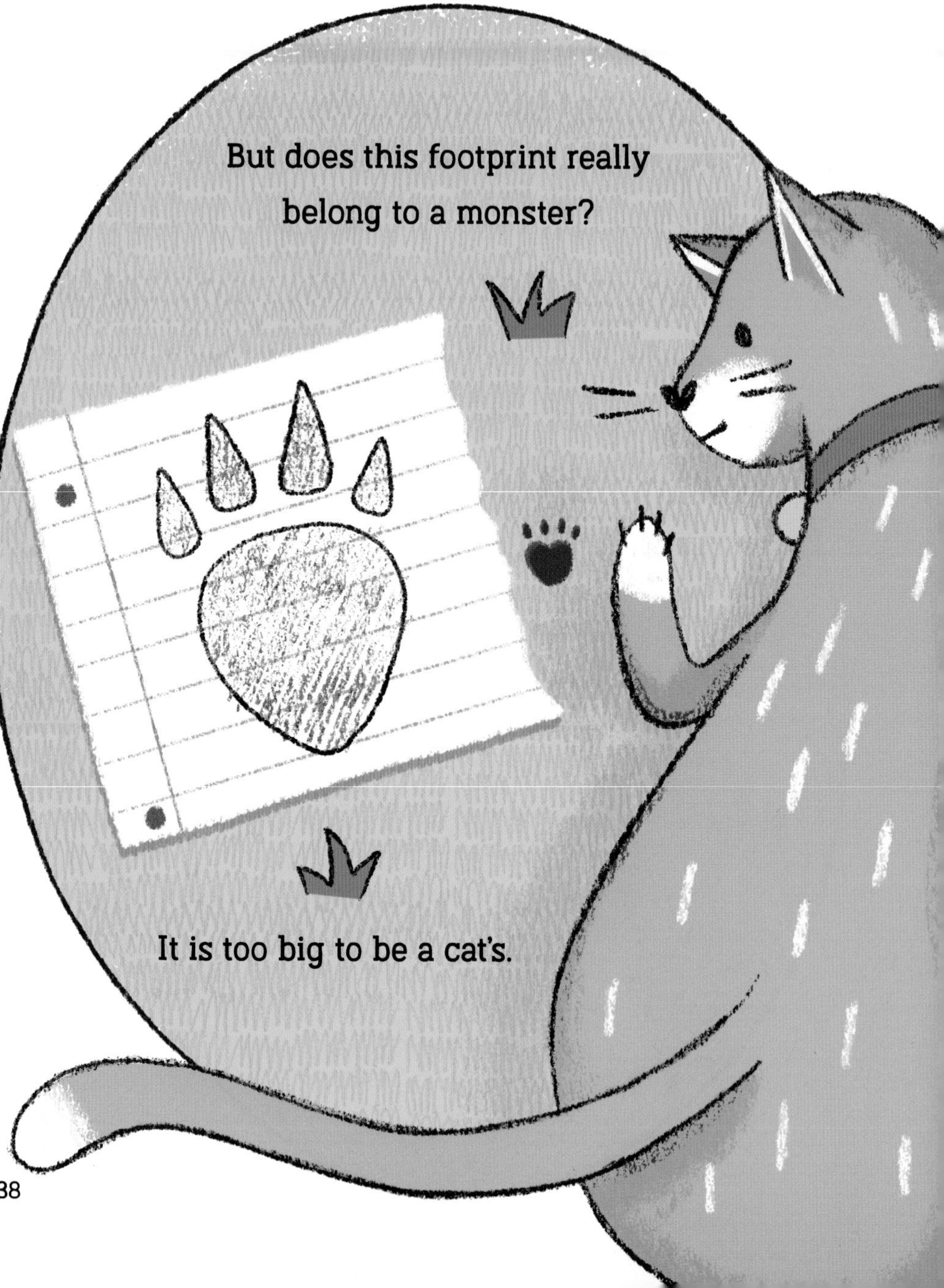

It is too big to be a cat's.

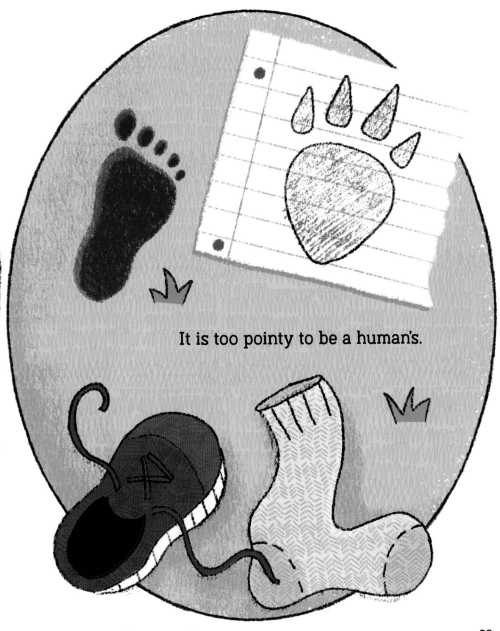

It is too pointy to be a human's.

39

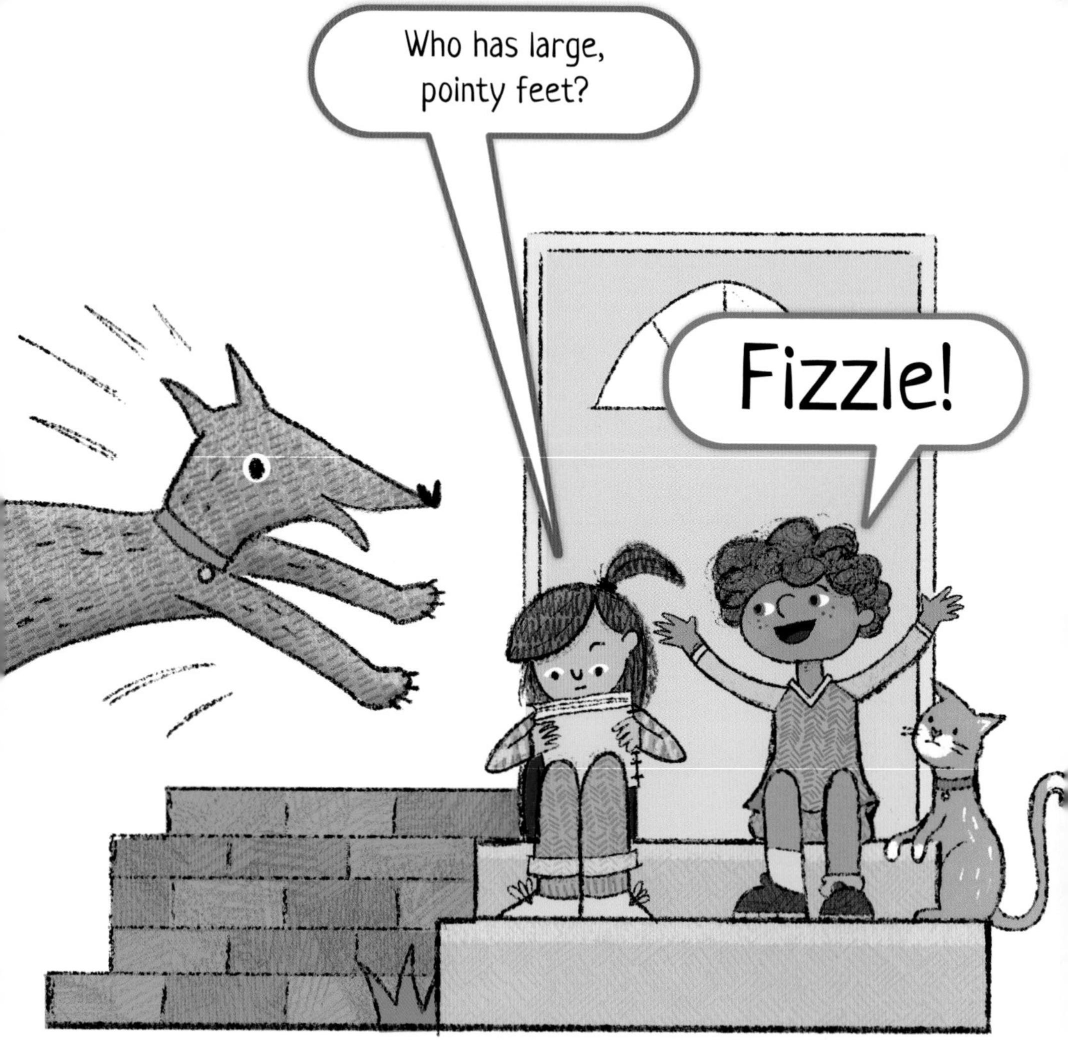
Who has large, pointy feet?
Fizzle!

Sometimes the facts jump right into your lap.

Name: Fizzle the dog

Breed: Scottish deerhound

Owner: Ms. M

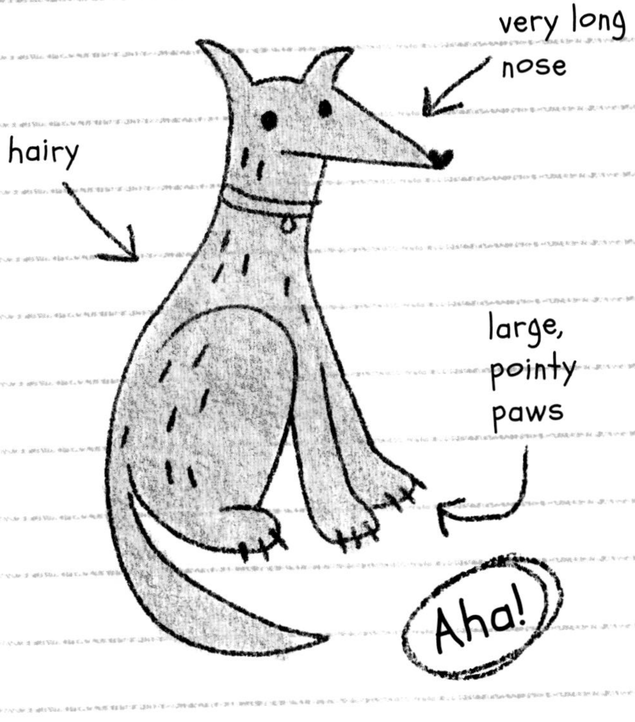
very long nose
hairy
large, pointy paws
Aha!

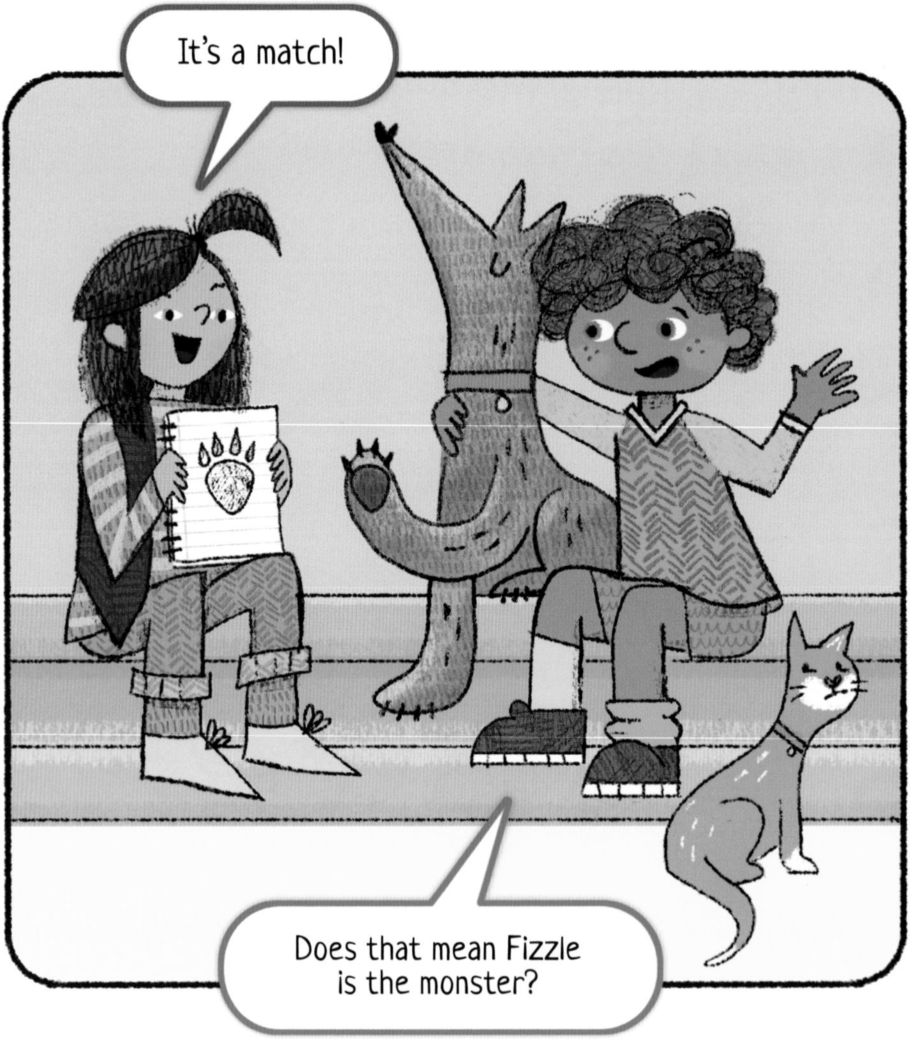
It’s a match!
Does that mean Fizzle is the monster?

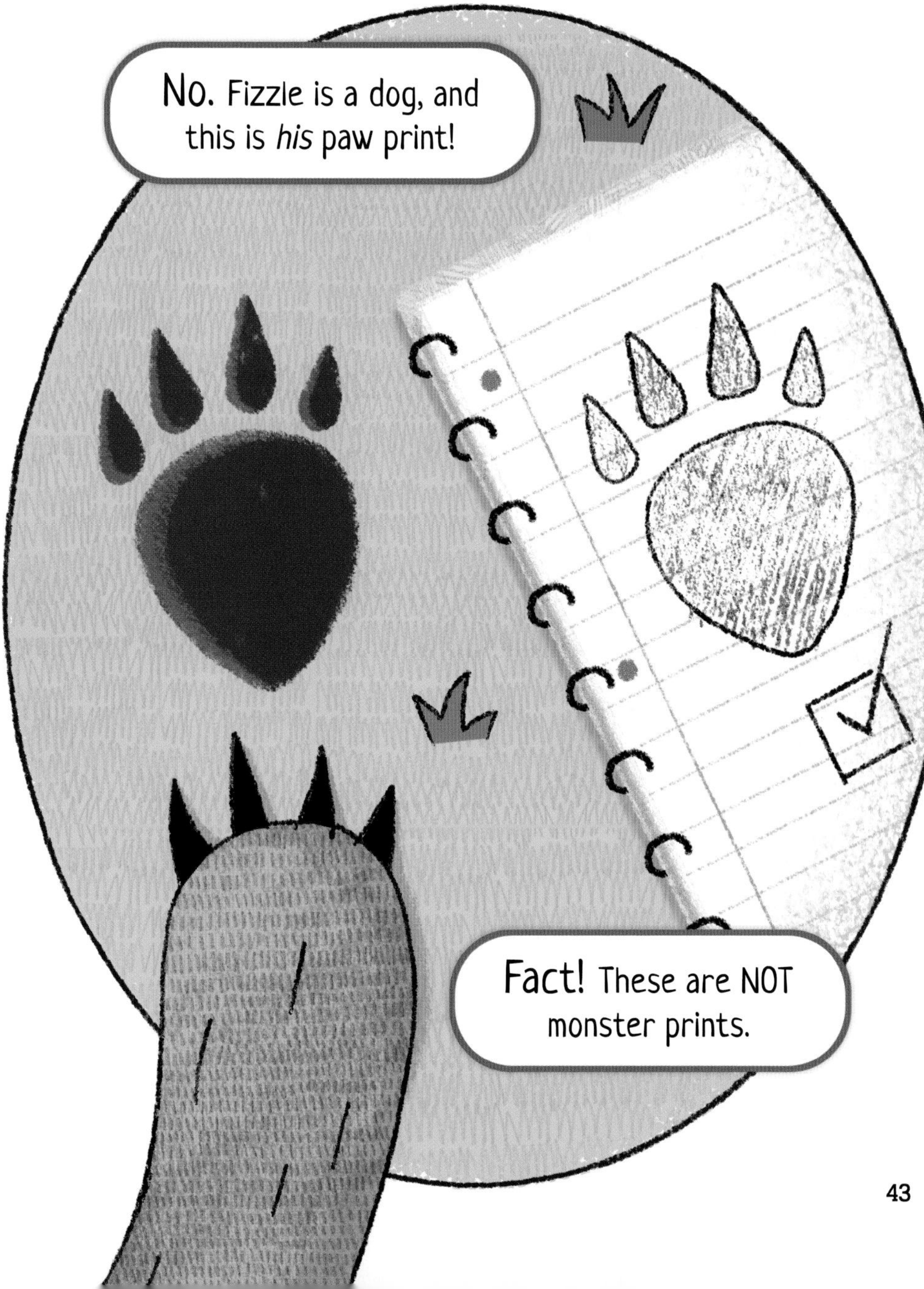
No. Fizzle is a dog, and this is *his* paw print!
Fact! These are NOT monster prints.

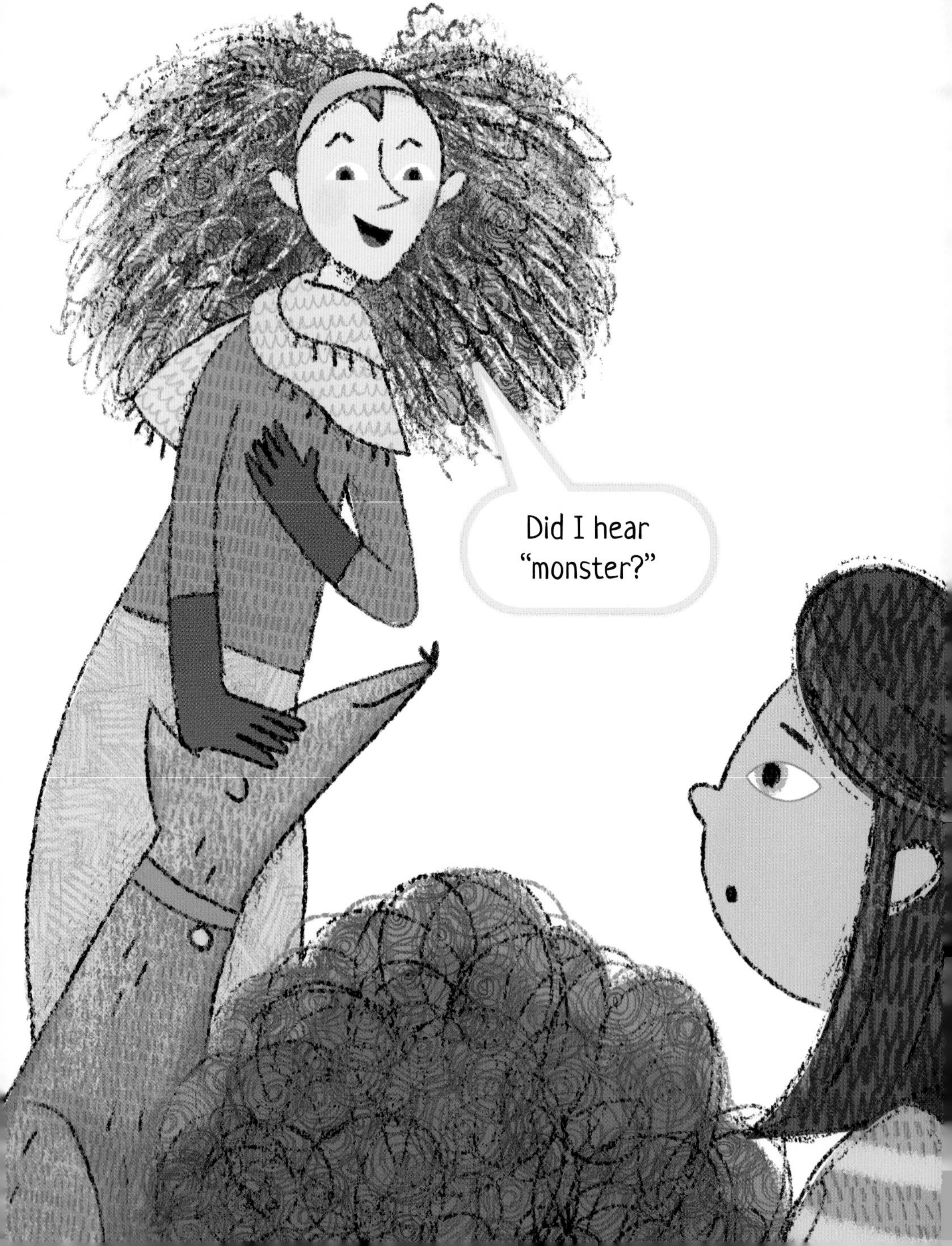
Did I hear "monster?"

Name: Ms. M

Fizzle's owner

wild hair!

always
wears
gloves

is friendly
to everyone

very tall

45

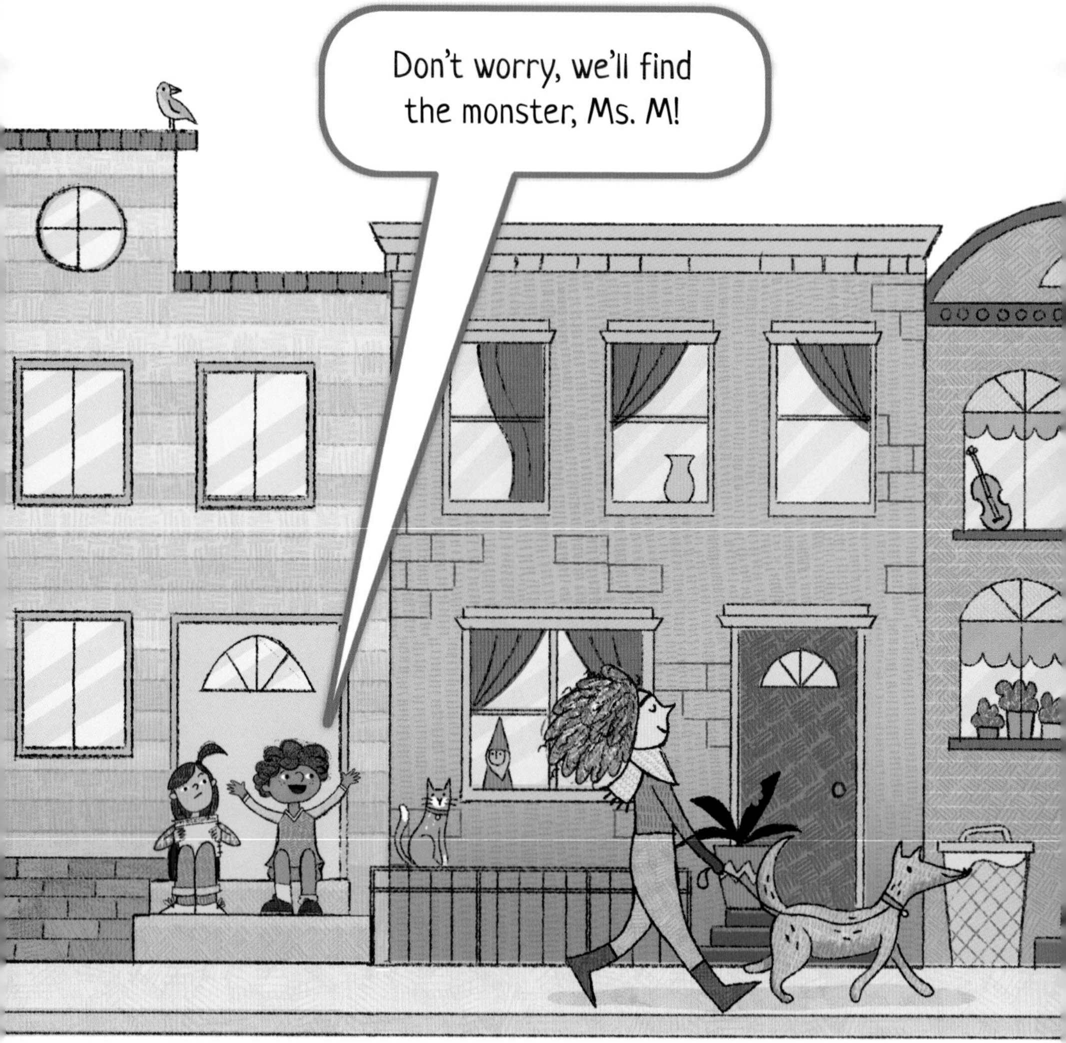
Don't worry, we'll find the monster, Ms. M!

Ms. M just laughs and gives us a wink before walking off with Fizzle.

MONSTER EVIDENCE:

~~leaves behind footprints~~

☑ dog paw prints   Fizzle's!

hides in the bushes

scary screeches

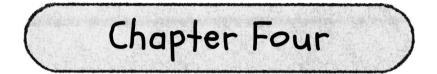

Chapter Four

Next, Penn and I walk down to the edge of the block.
Penn points at a leafy bush on the corner.

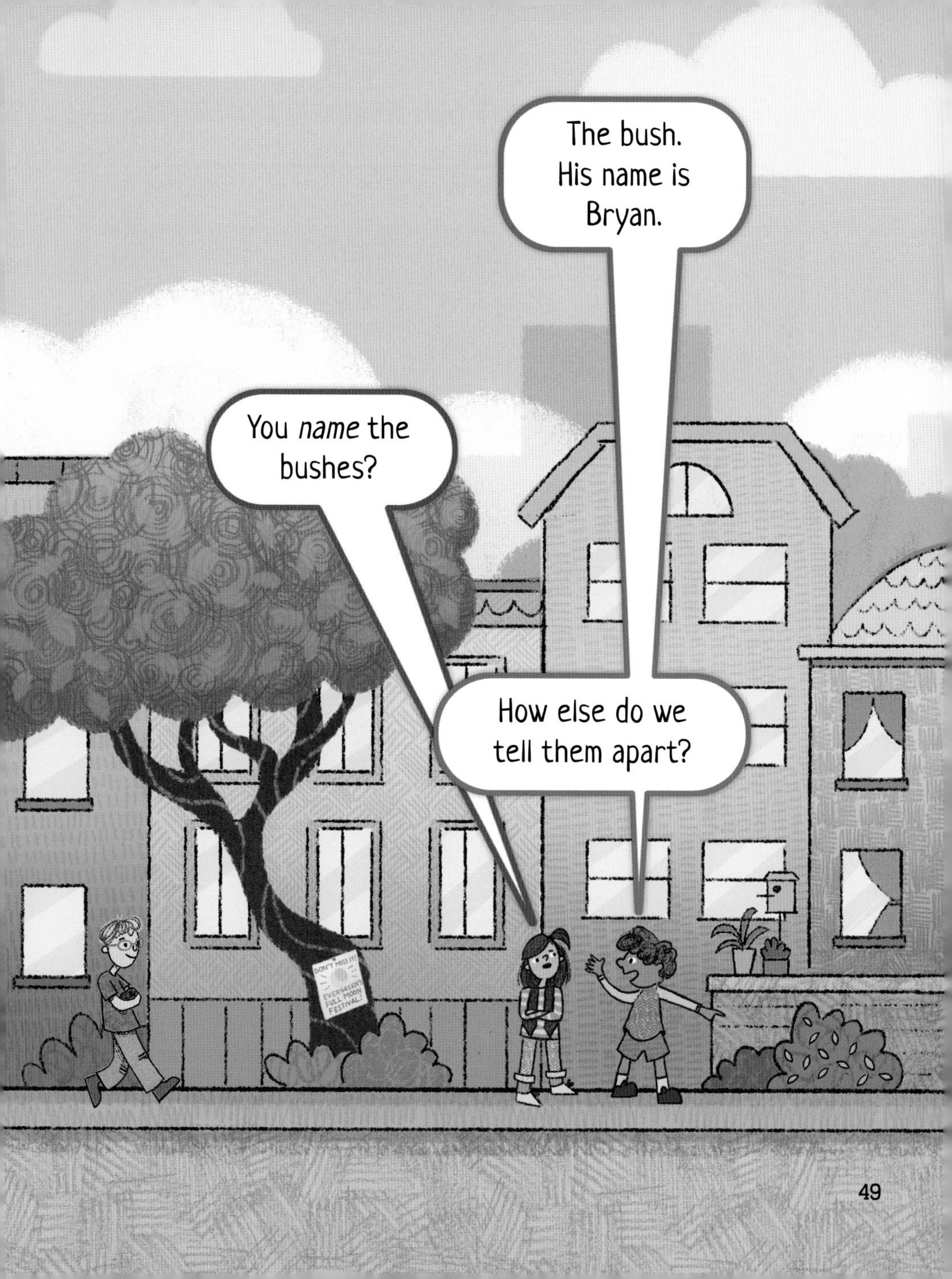
You *name* the bushes?
The bush. His name is Bryan.
How else do we tell them apart?
DON'T MISS IT!
EVERGREEN'S FULL MOON FESTIVAL!

To me, Bryan looks like a normal bush.

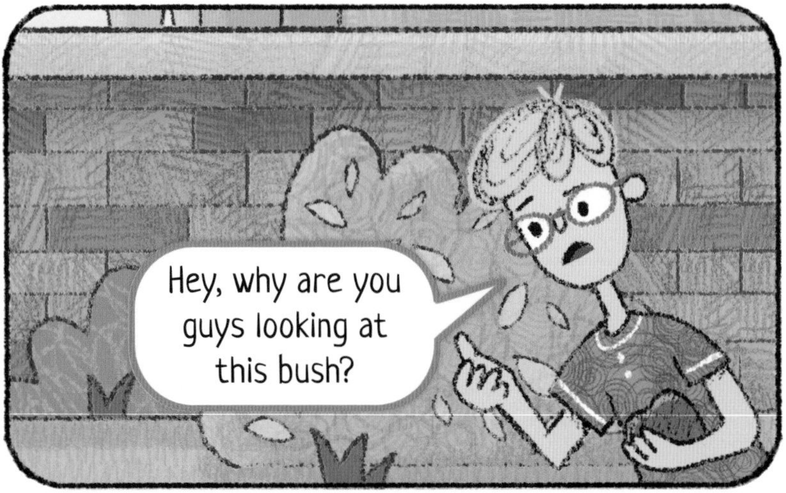
Hey, why are you guys looking at this bush?

But then Bryan starts to shake.

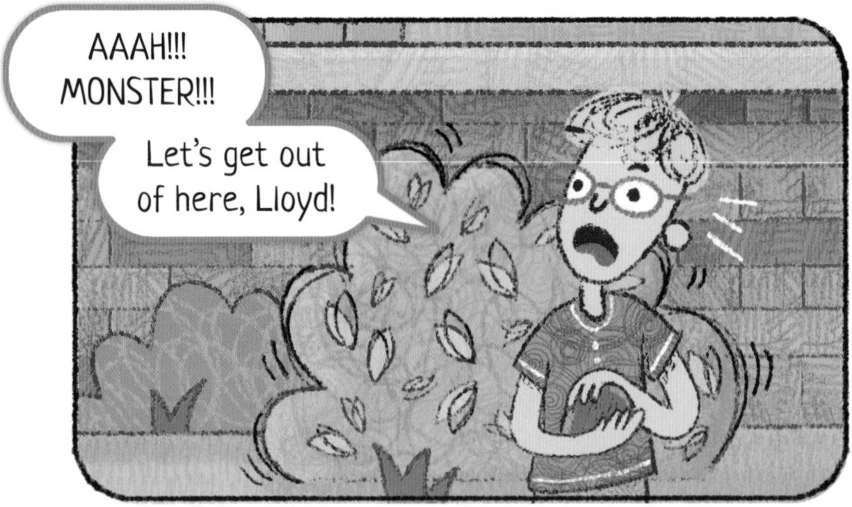
AAAH!!! MONSTER!!!
Let's get out of here, Lloyd!

Could a monster really be hiding in the bush?

There is only one way to find out.

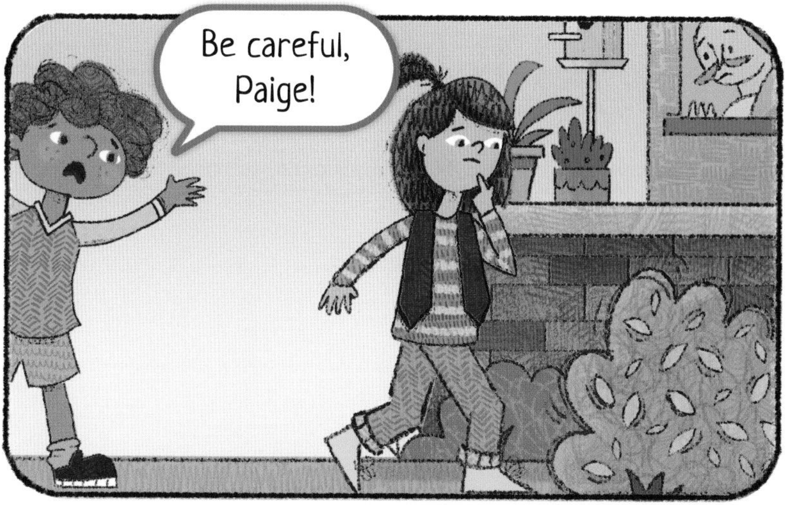
Be careful, Paige!

I take a deep breath and push aside the leaves. . . .

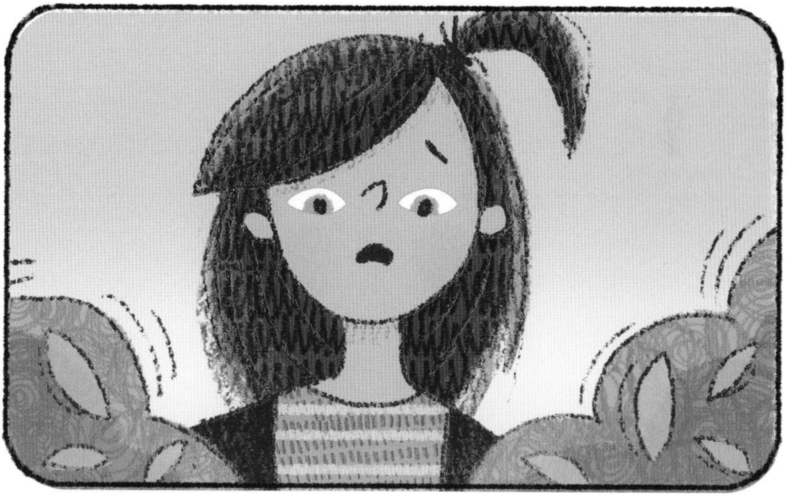

CHIRP-CHIRP-SQUAWK-CHIRP

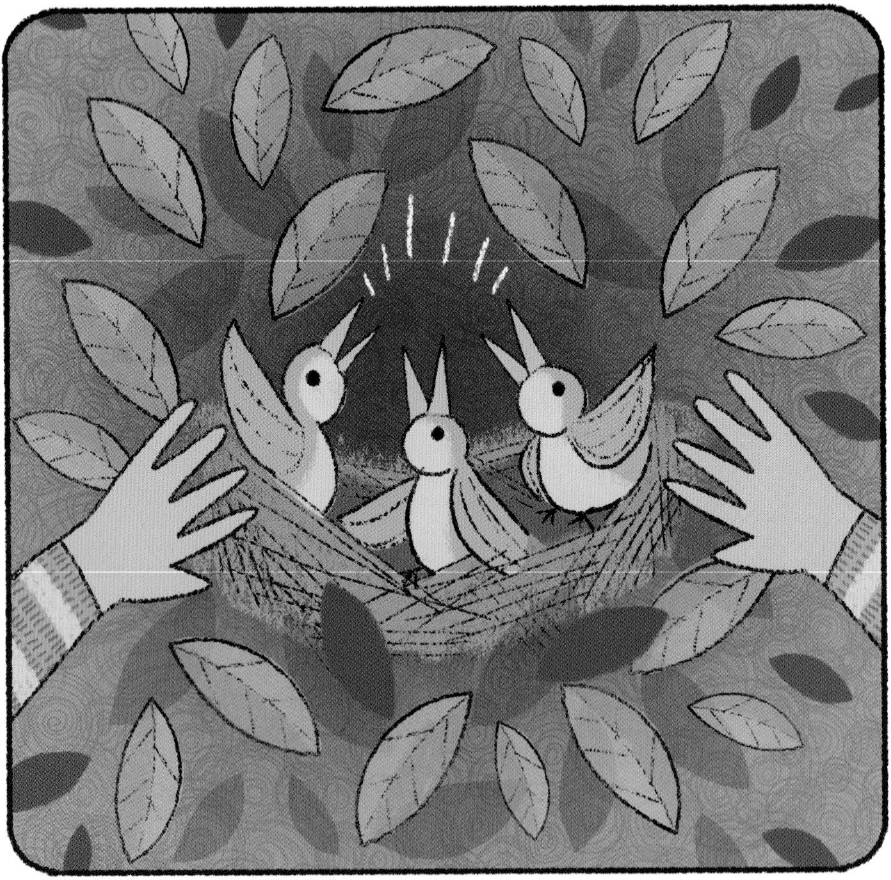

Baby birds! A whole nest of them!

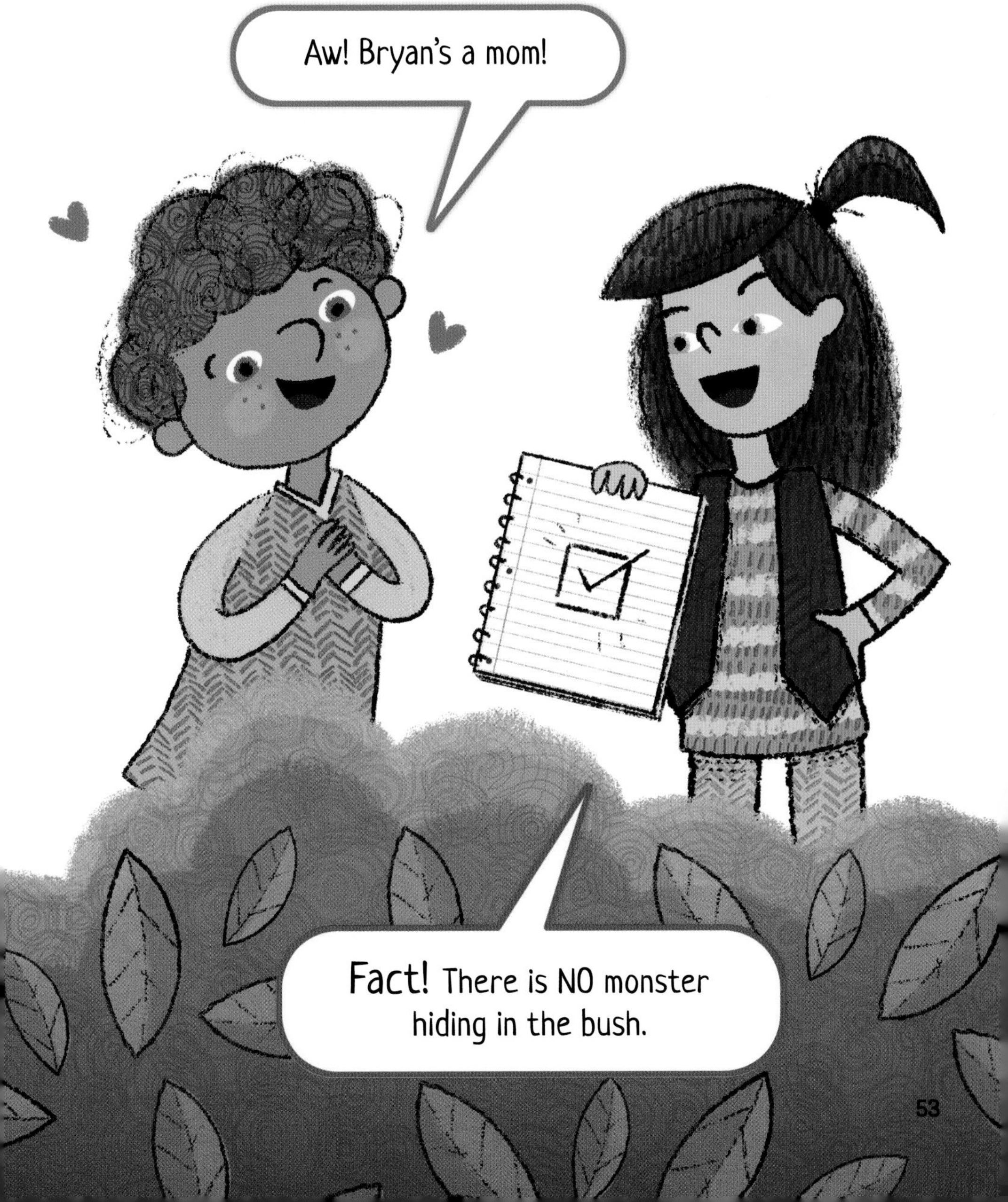
Aw! Bryan's a mom!
Fact! There is NO monster hiding in the bush.

This is Mr. Drufus.

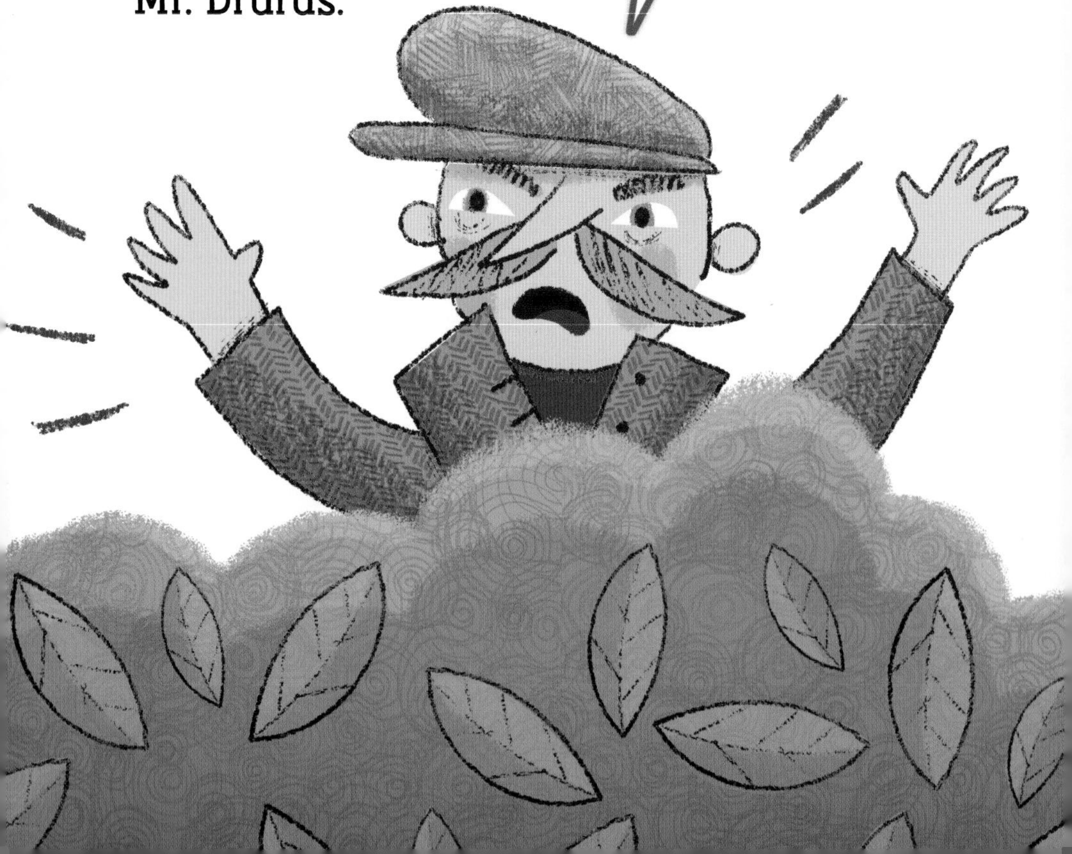
Of course there isn't! That's a rare family of willow warblers!
Please show some respect for these fine feathery creatures and give them some space!

Name: Mr. Drufus

lives on the corner
of Evergreen Street

only likes birds

very grumpy!

wears a hat

always has birdseed
in his pockets

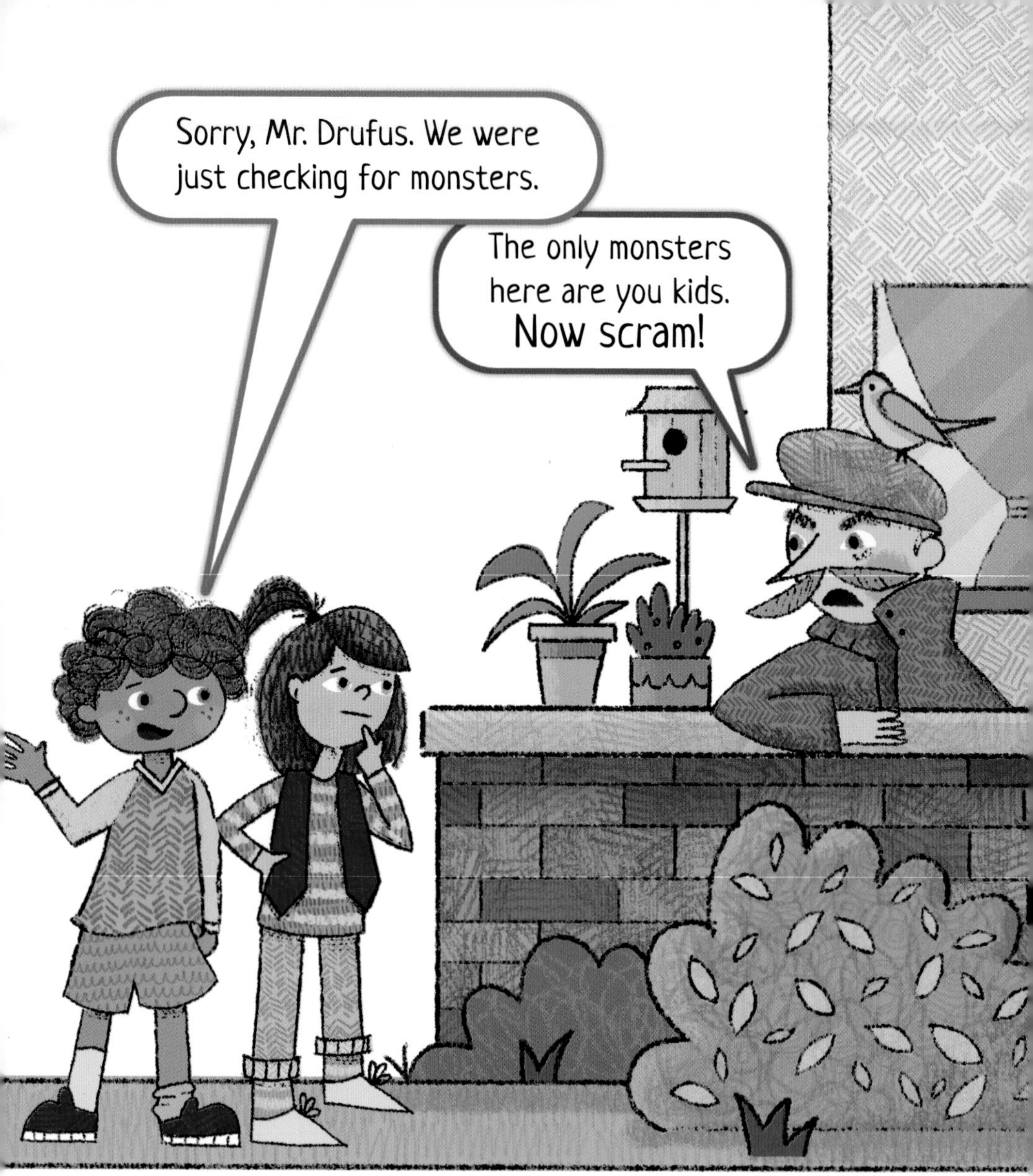
Sorry, Mr. Drufus. We were just checking for monsters.
The only monsters here are you kids. Now scram!

He's not a fan of kids.

MONSTER EVIDENCE:

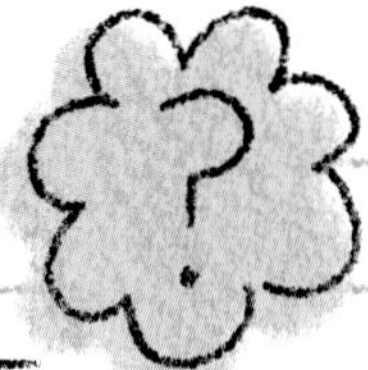

- ~~leaves behind footprints~~

☑ dog paw prints 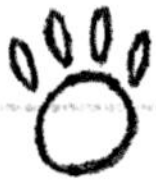 Fizzle's!

- ~~hides in the bushes~~

☑ bird's nest 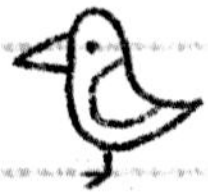 Baby Birds

- Scary screeches

Chapter Five

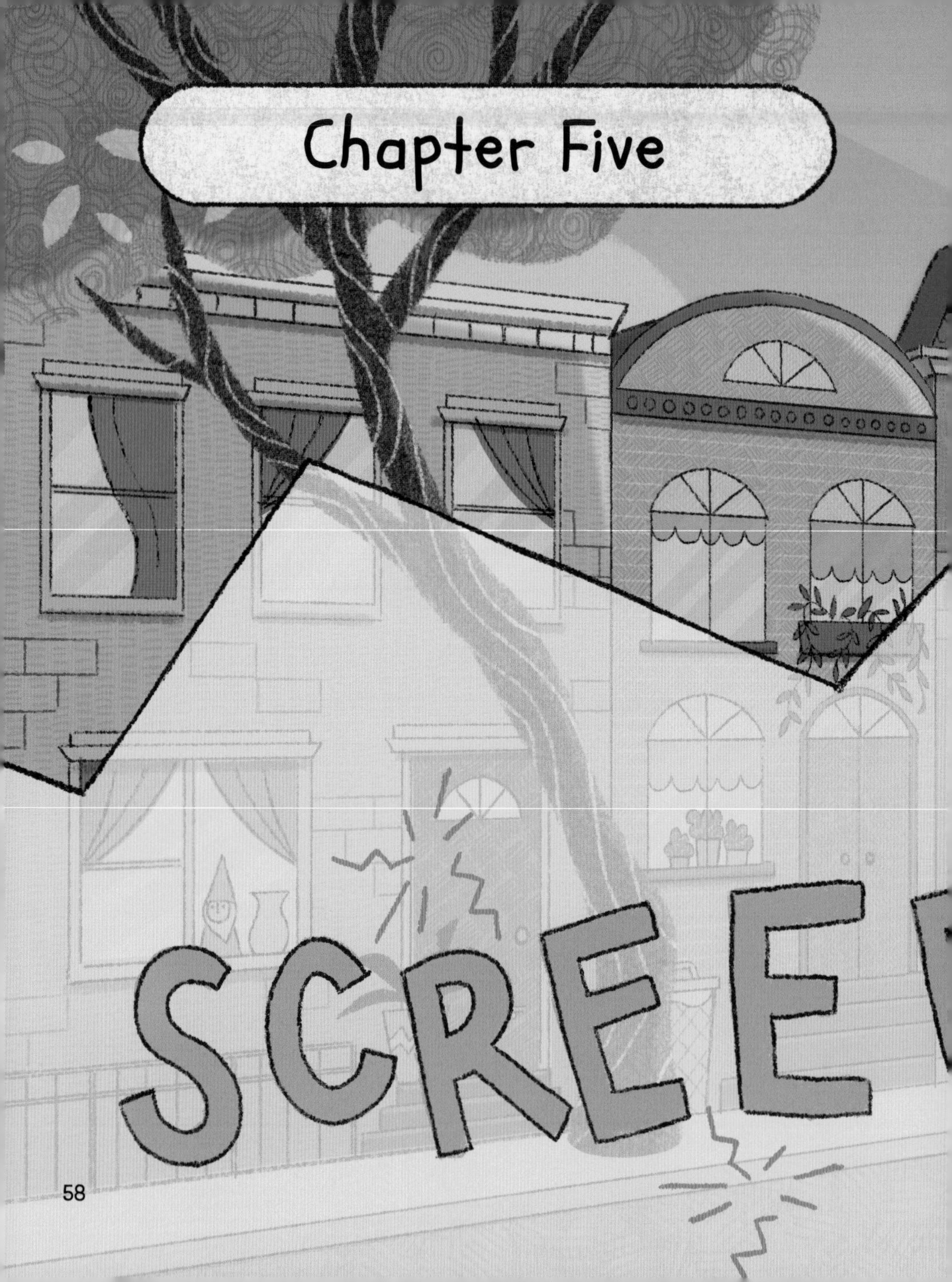
SCREE

So far, none of the evidence has proven there is a monster. But we have one more investigation: scary screeches. Sure enough, when the sun is setting, there is a sudden screeching noise. It is horrible.

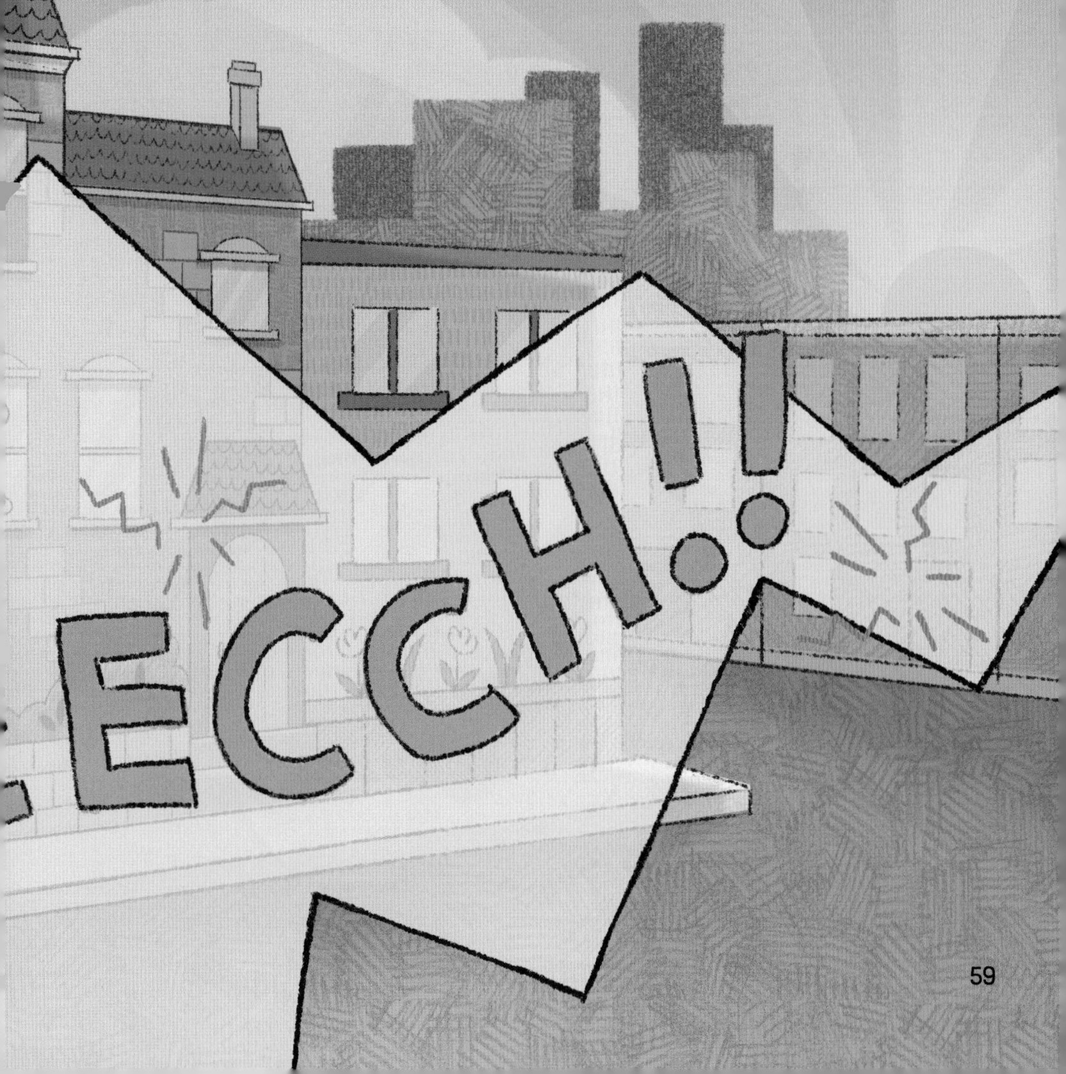
ECCH!!

Is it someone moving patio furniture?

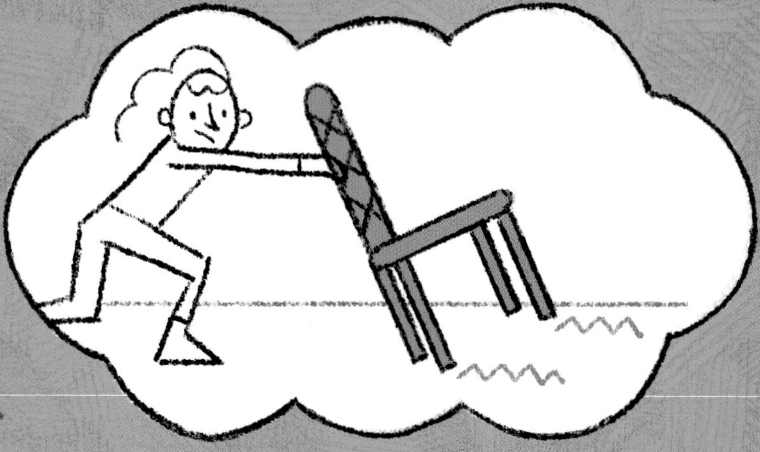

Or starting up a lawn mower?

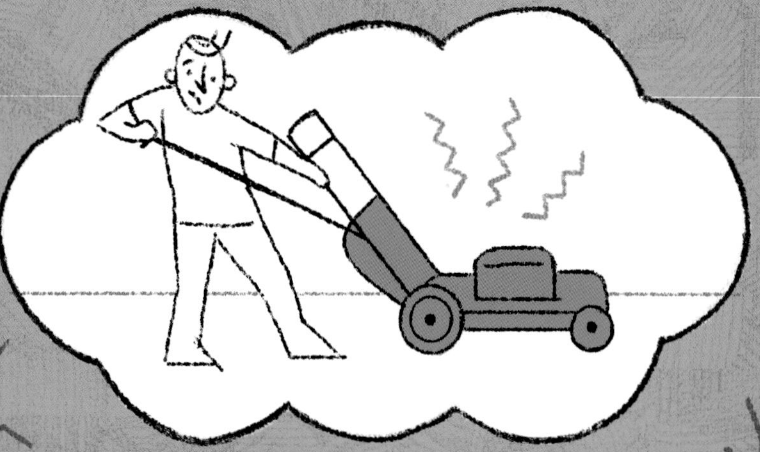

Or the creaking of an old rusty gate?

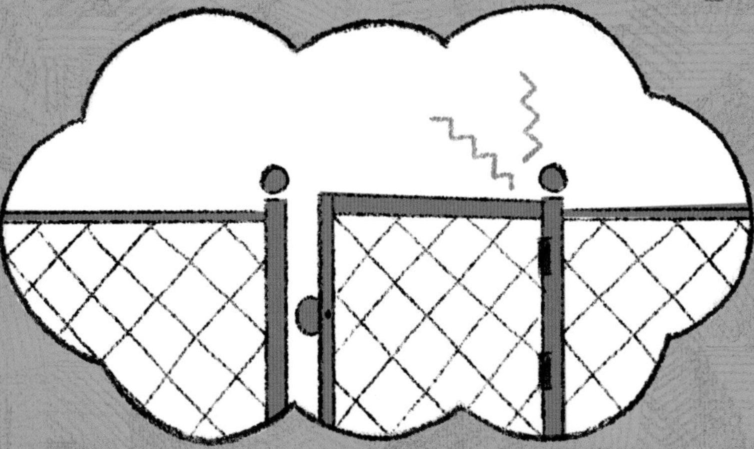

Or could it really be the scary screeching of a monster?!

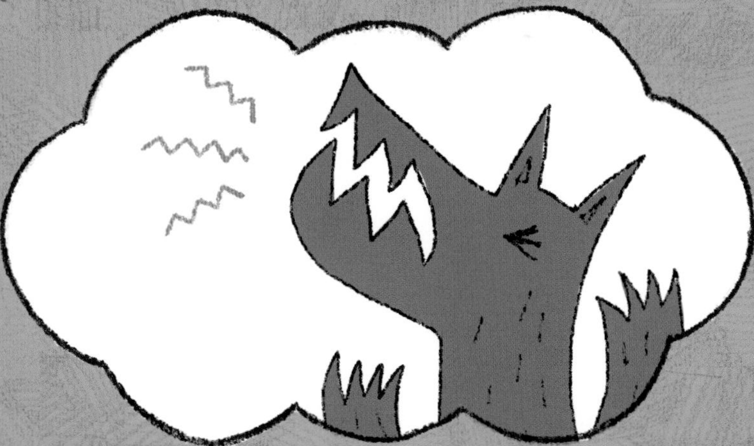

But my dad says, "Don't believe everything you hear."
So we had to find out where this noise was coming from.

Was it the mailbox?

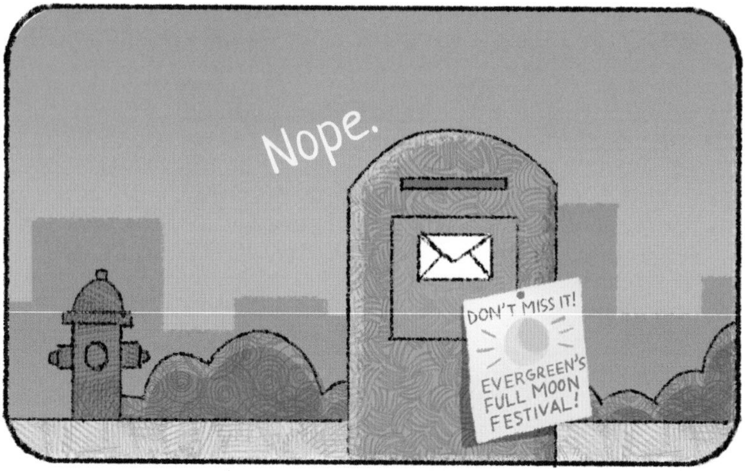
Nope.
DON'T MISS IT!
EVERGREEN'S FULL MOON FESTIVAL!

Was it the trashcan?

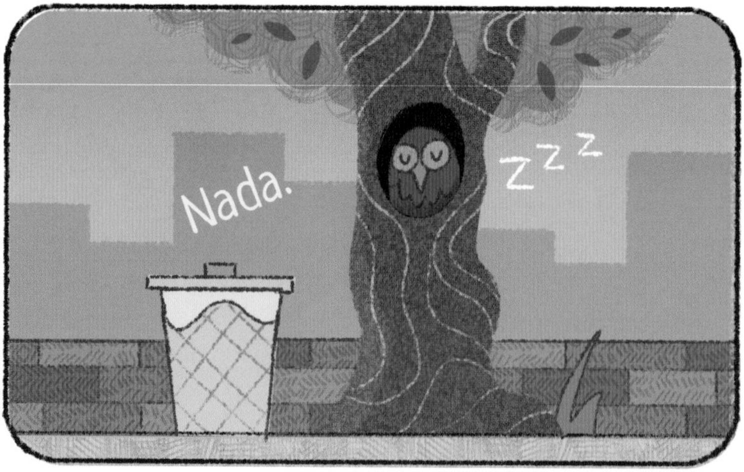
Nada.
Z Z Z

Was it the pet rock?

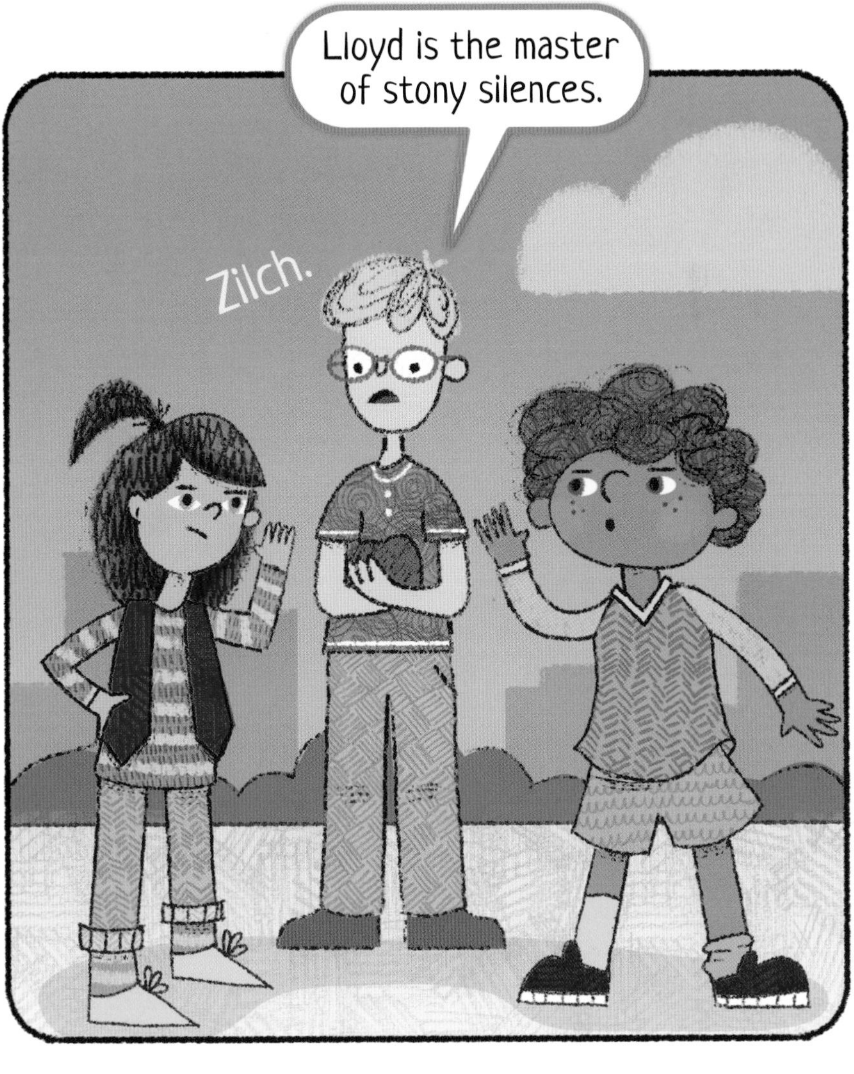
Lloyd is the master of stony silences.
Zilch.

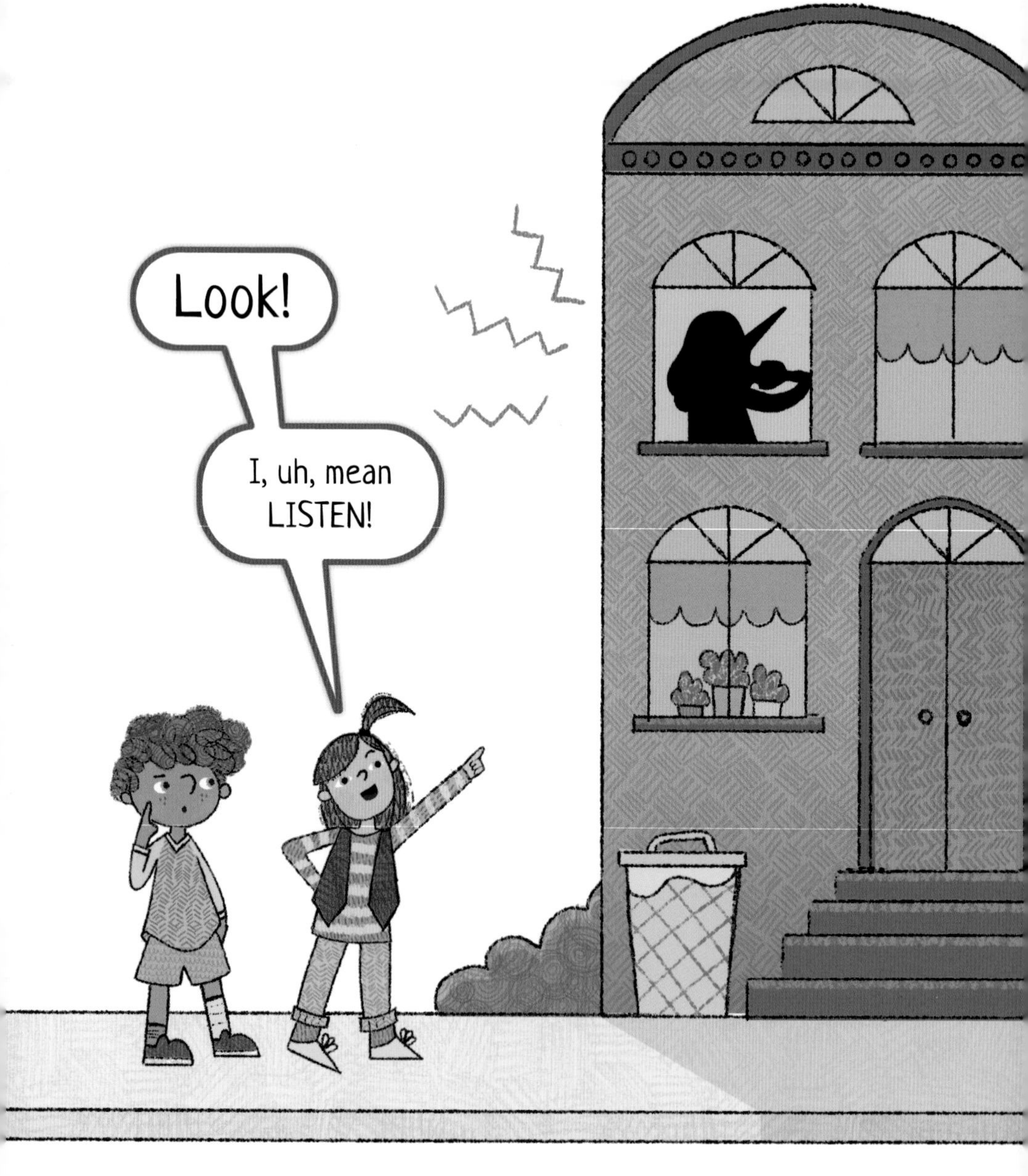
Look!
I, uh, mean LISTEN!

It looks like a monster!

It sounds like a monster!

But is it?

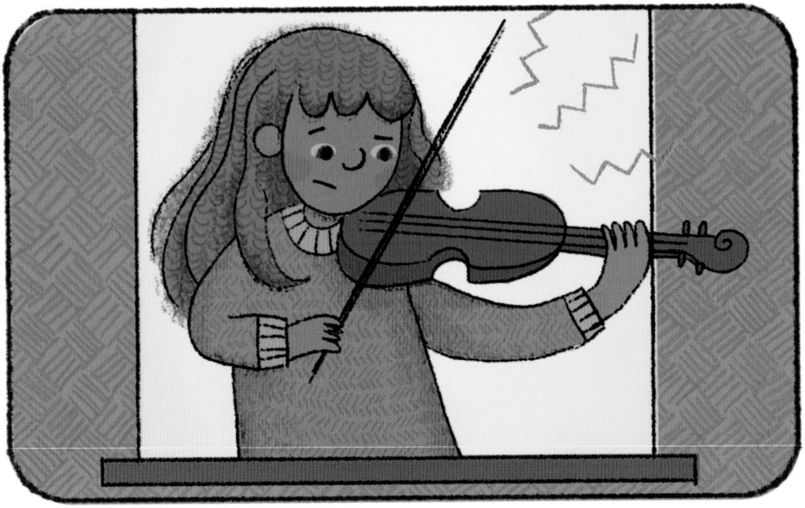

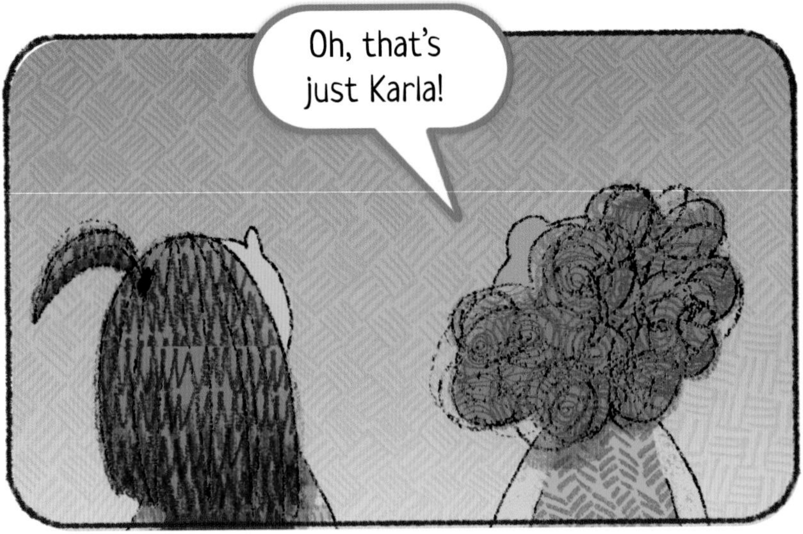
Oh, that's just Karla!

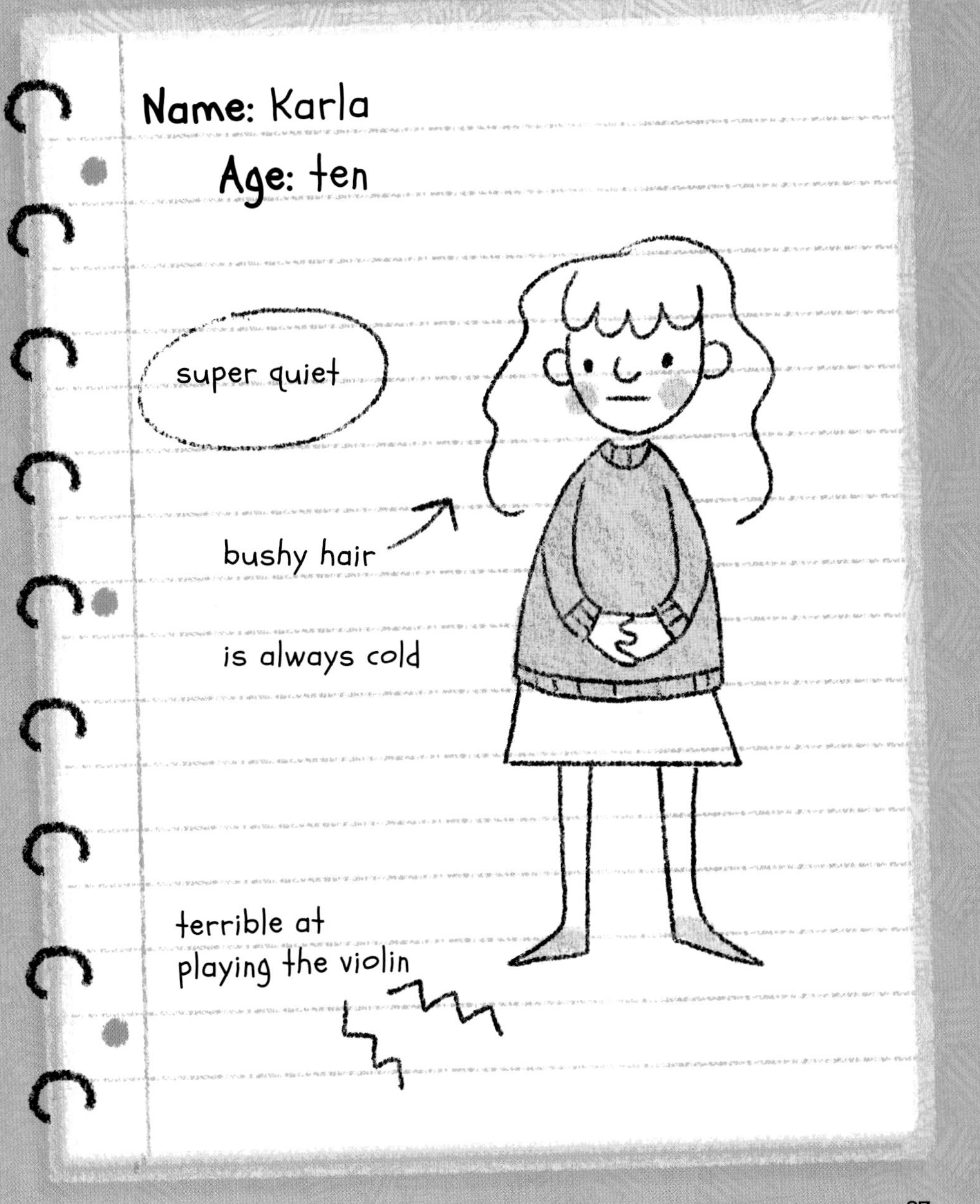
Name: Karla
Age: ten
super quiet
bushy hair
is always cold
terrible at
playing the violin

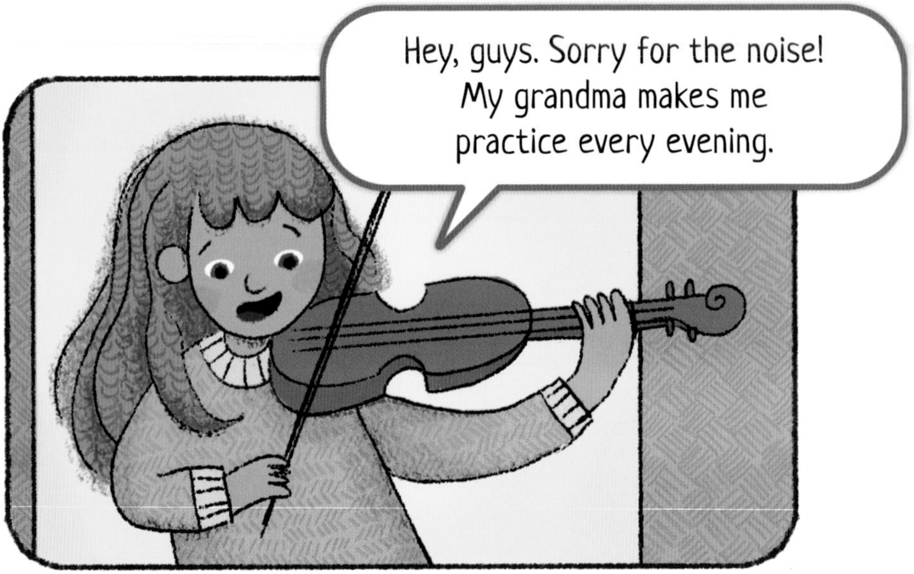
Hey, guys. Sorry for the noise! My grandma makes me practice every evening.

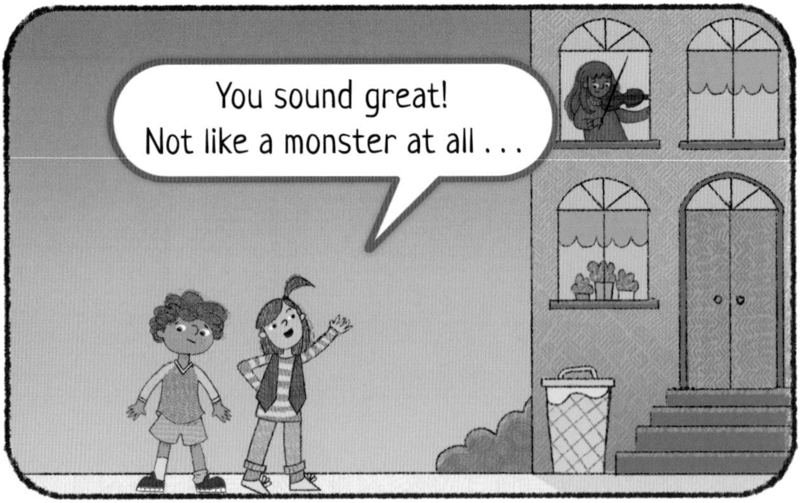
You sound great! Not like a monster at all . . .

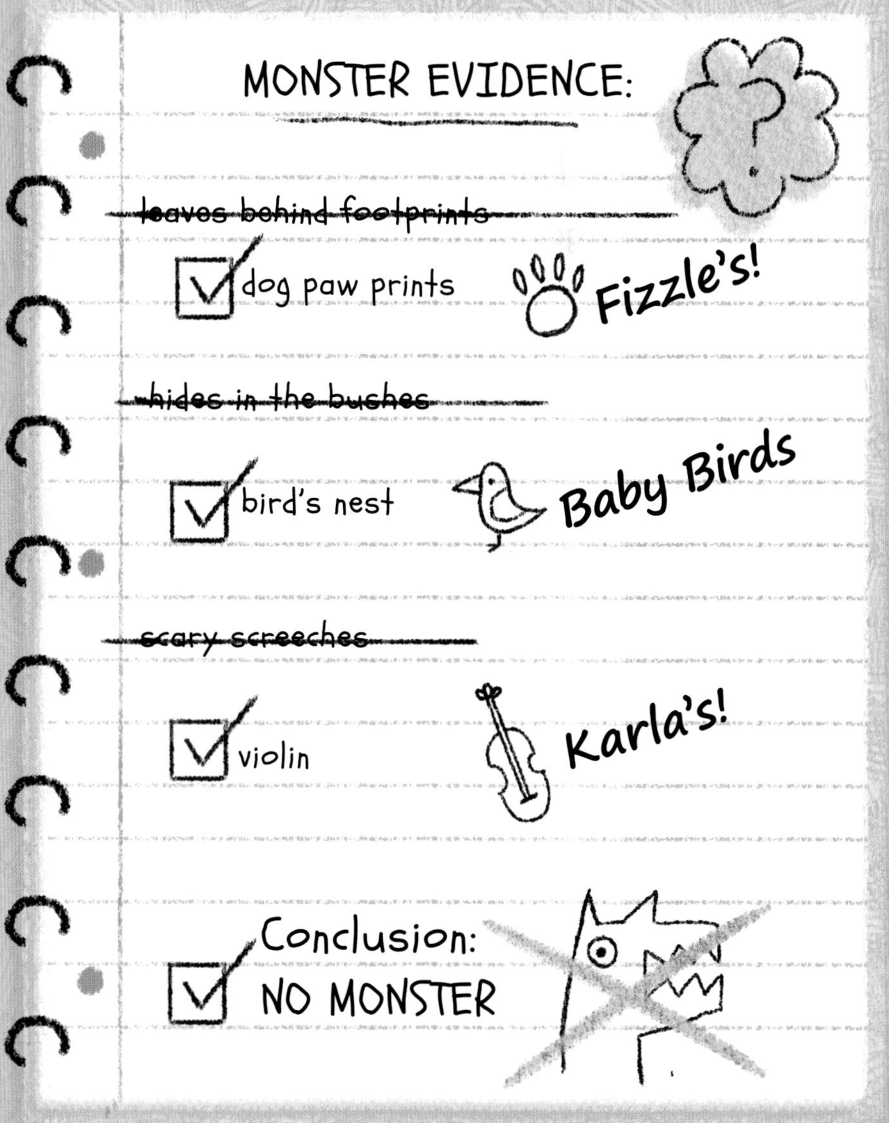
MONSTER EVIDENCE:
?
~~leaves behind footprints~~
dog paw prints
Fizzle's!
~~hides in the bushes~~
bird's nest
Baby Birds
~~scary screeches~~
violin
Karla's!
Conclusion:
NO MONSTER

Chapter Six

I have done it!

I, Paige, have proven a fact!

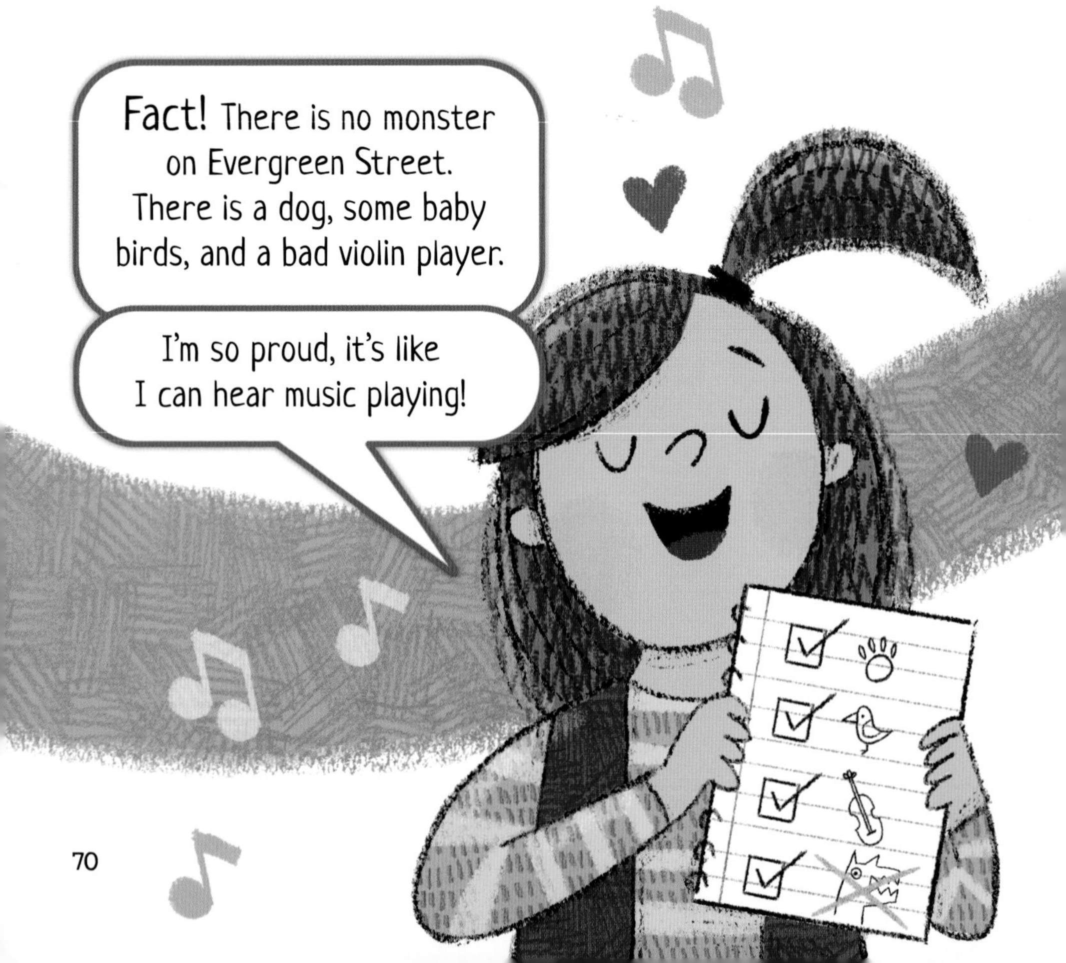

Fact! There is no monster on Evergreen Street. There is a dog, some baby birds, and a bad violin player.
I'm so proud, it's like I can hear music playing!

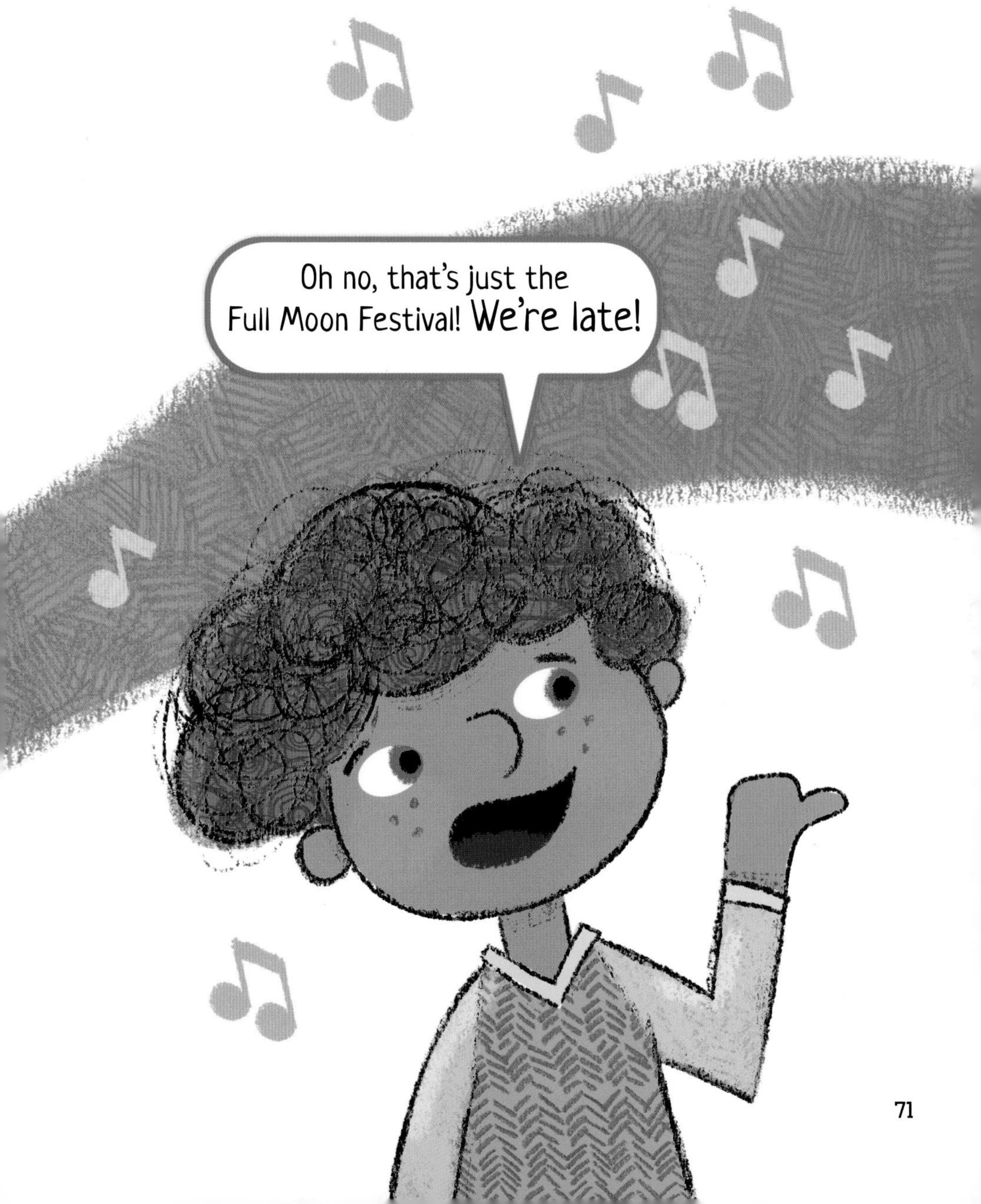
Oh no, that's just the Full Moon Festival! We're late!

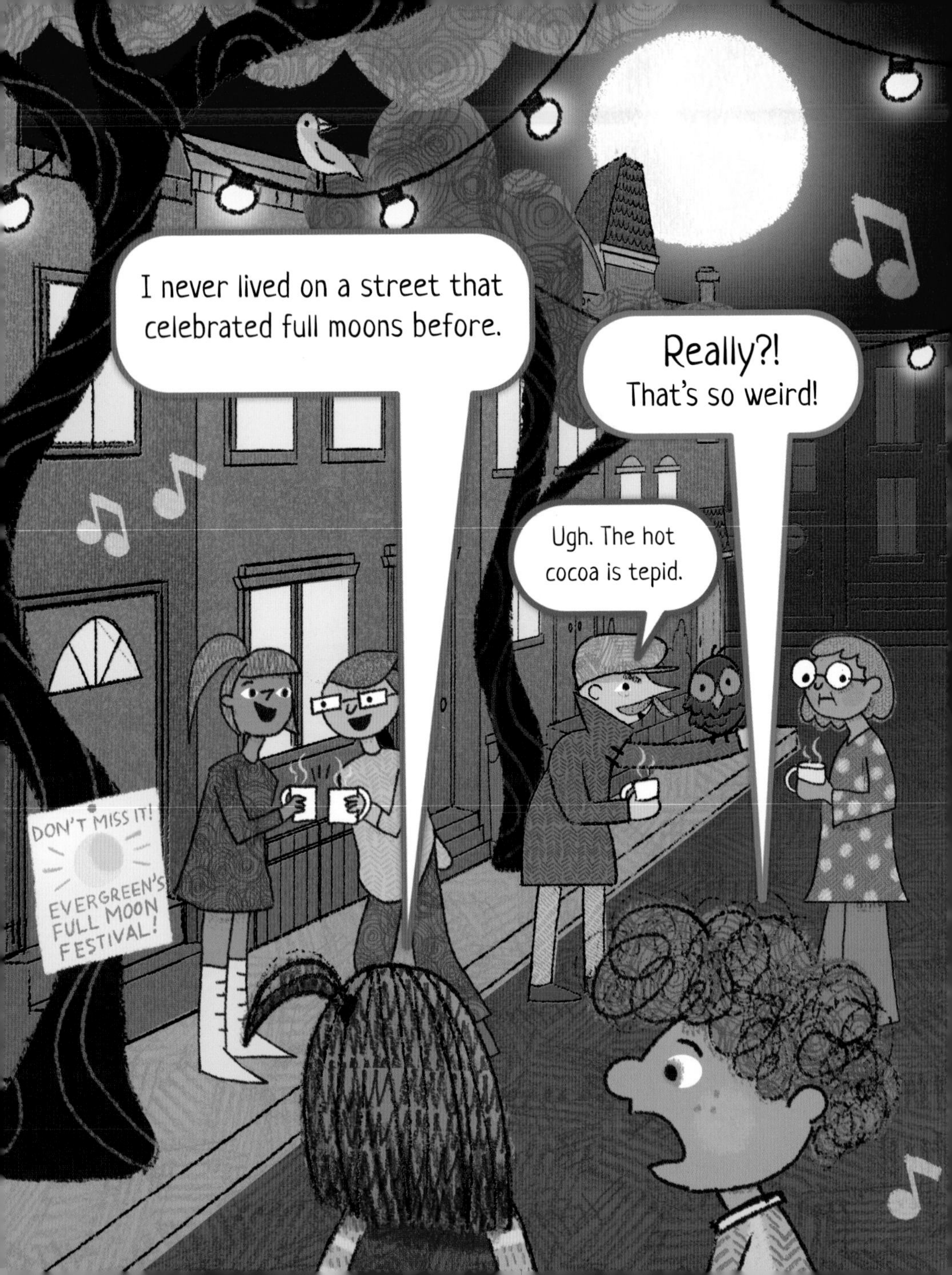
I never lived on a street that celebrated full moons before.
Really?! That's so weird!
Ugh. The hot cocoa is tepid.
DON'T MISS IT!
EVERGREEN'S FULL MOON FESTIVAL!

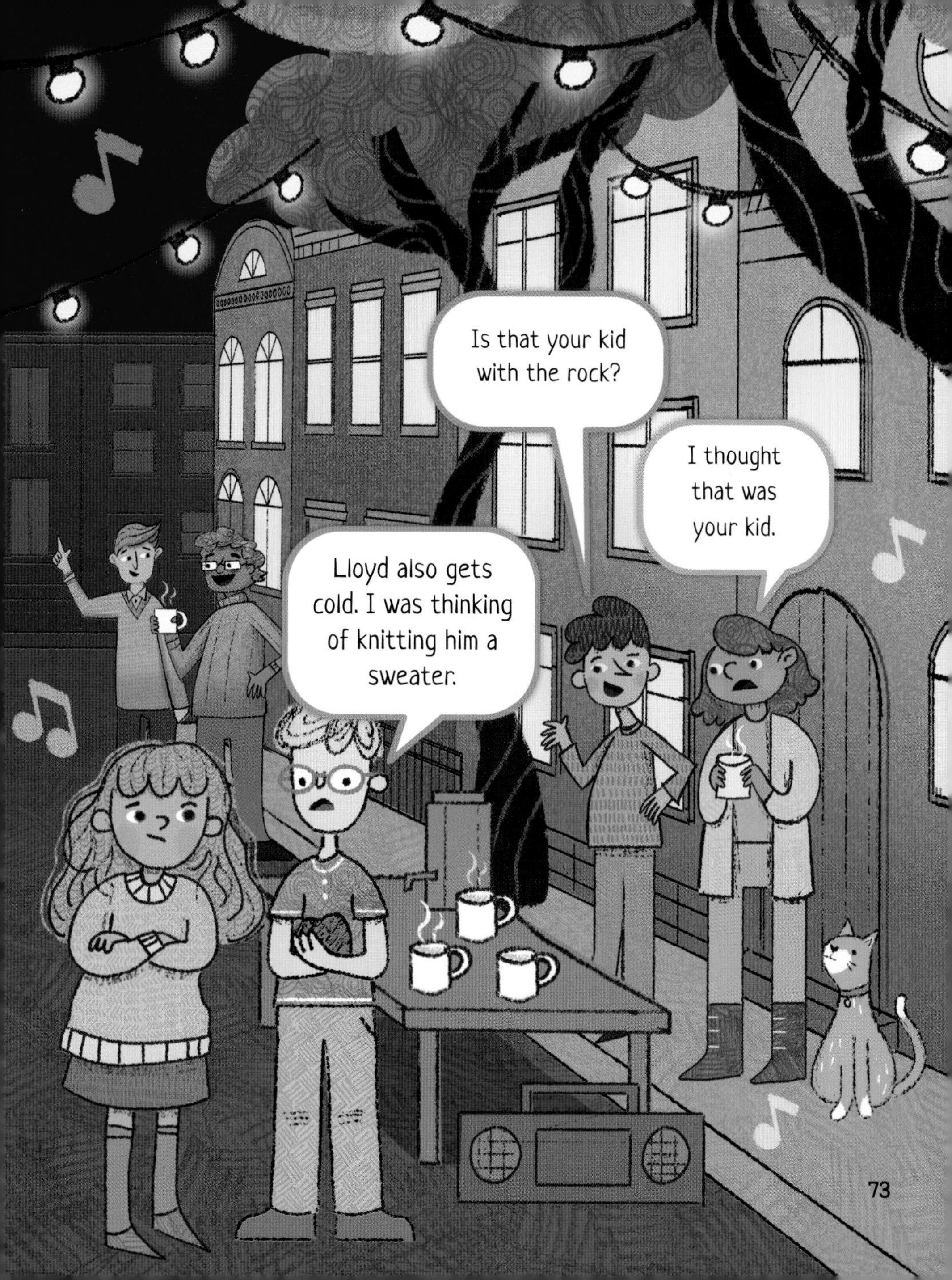
Is that your kid with the rock?
I thought that was your kid.
Lloyd also gets cold. I was thinking of knitting him a sweater.

I had just gotten a cup of hot cocoa when . . .

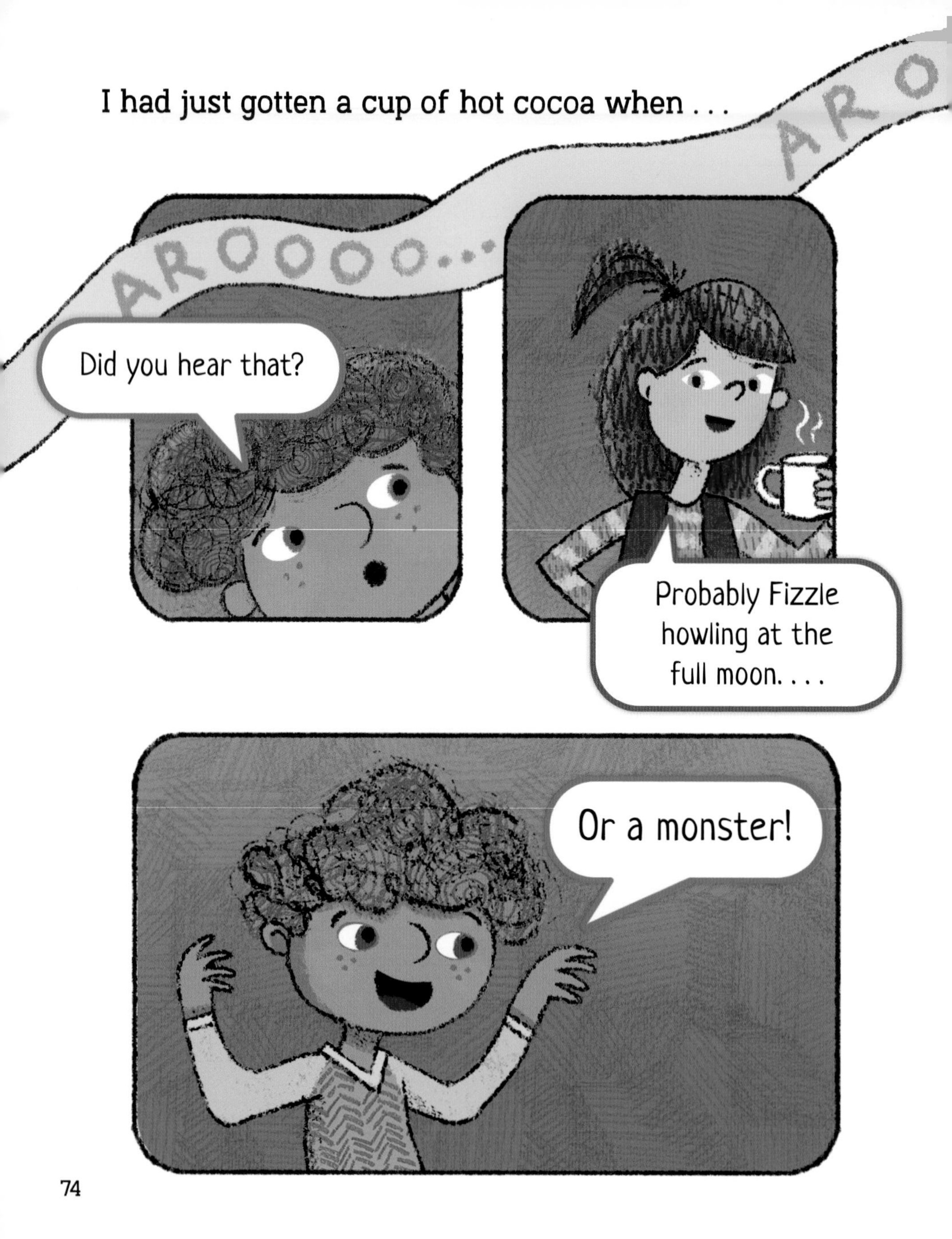
AROOOO...
Did you hear that?
Probably Fizzle howling at the full moon. . . .
Or a monster!

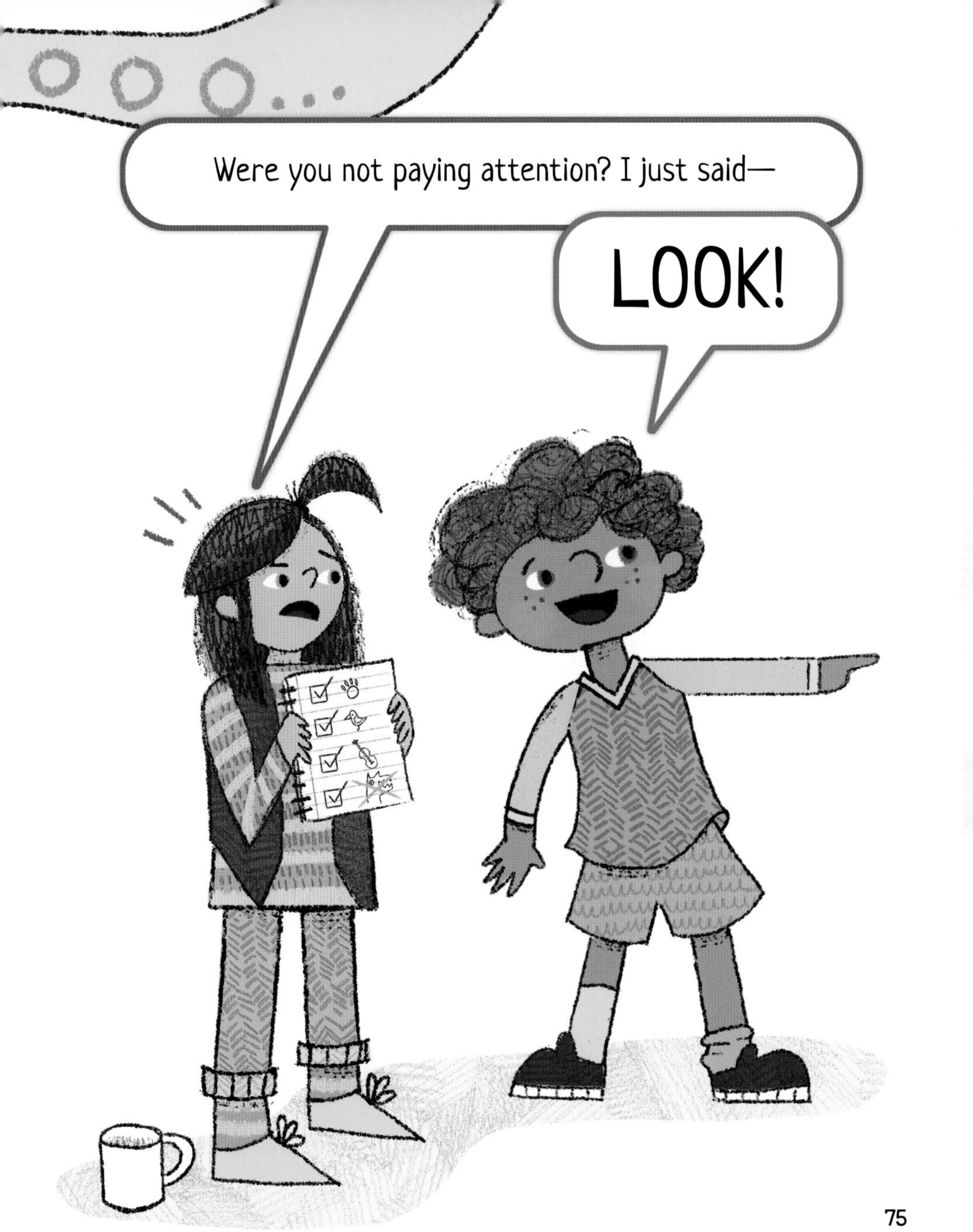
Were you not paying attention? I just said—
LOOK!

There is a strange shadow in the alley!

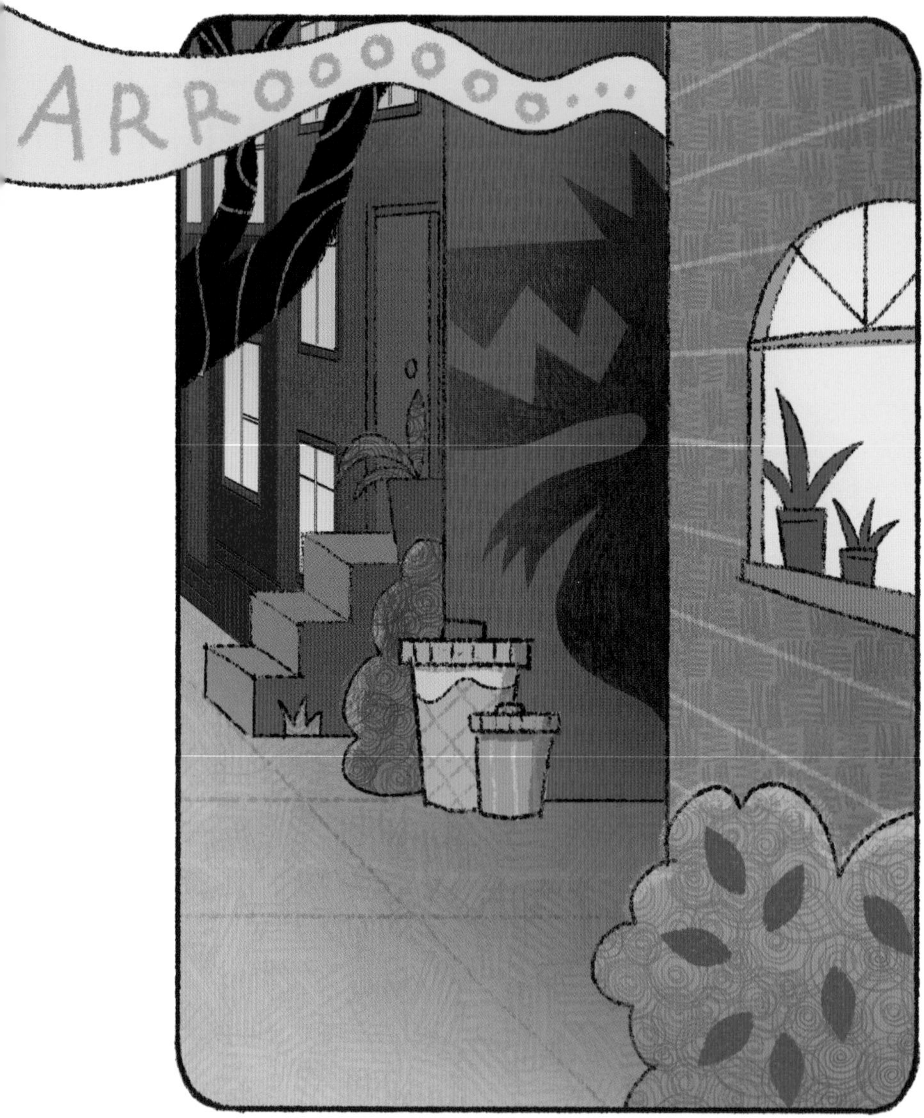
ARROOOOOOO...

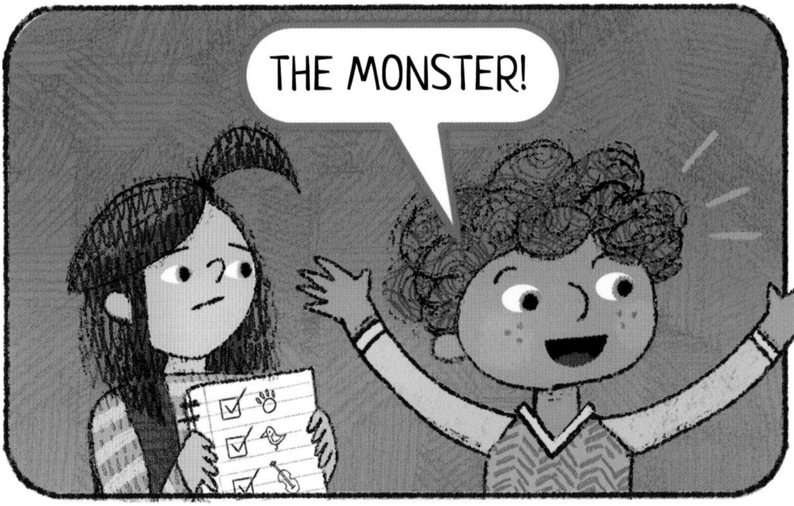
THE MONSTER!

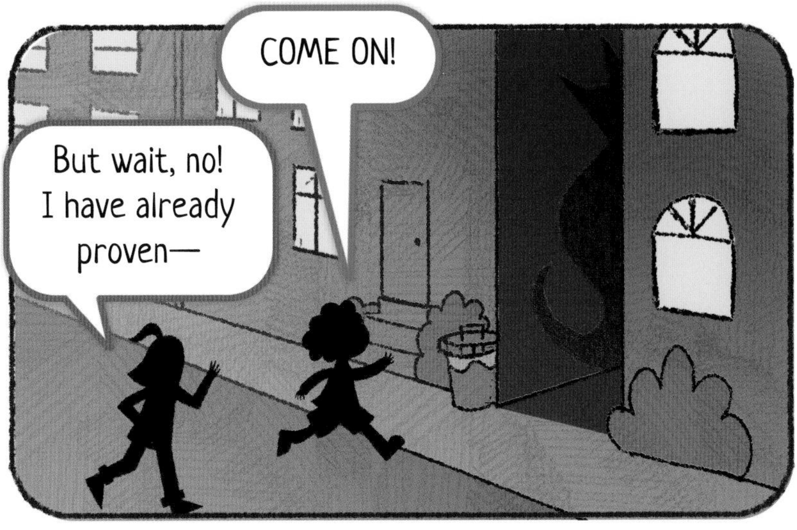
COME ON!
But wait, no! I have already proven—

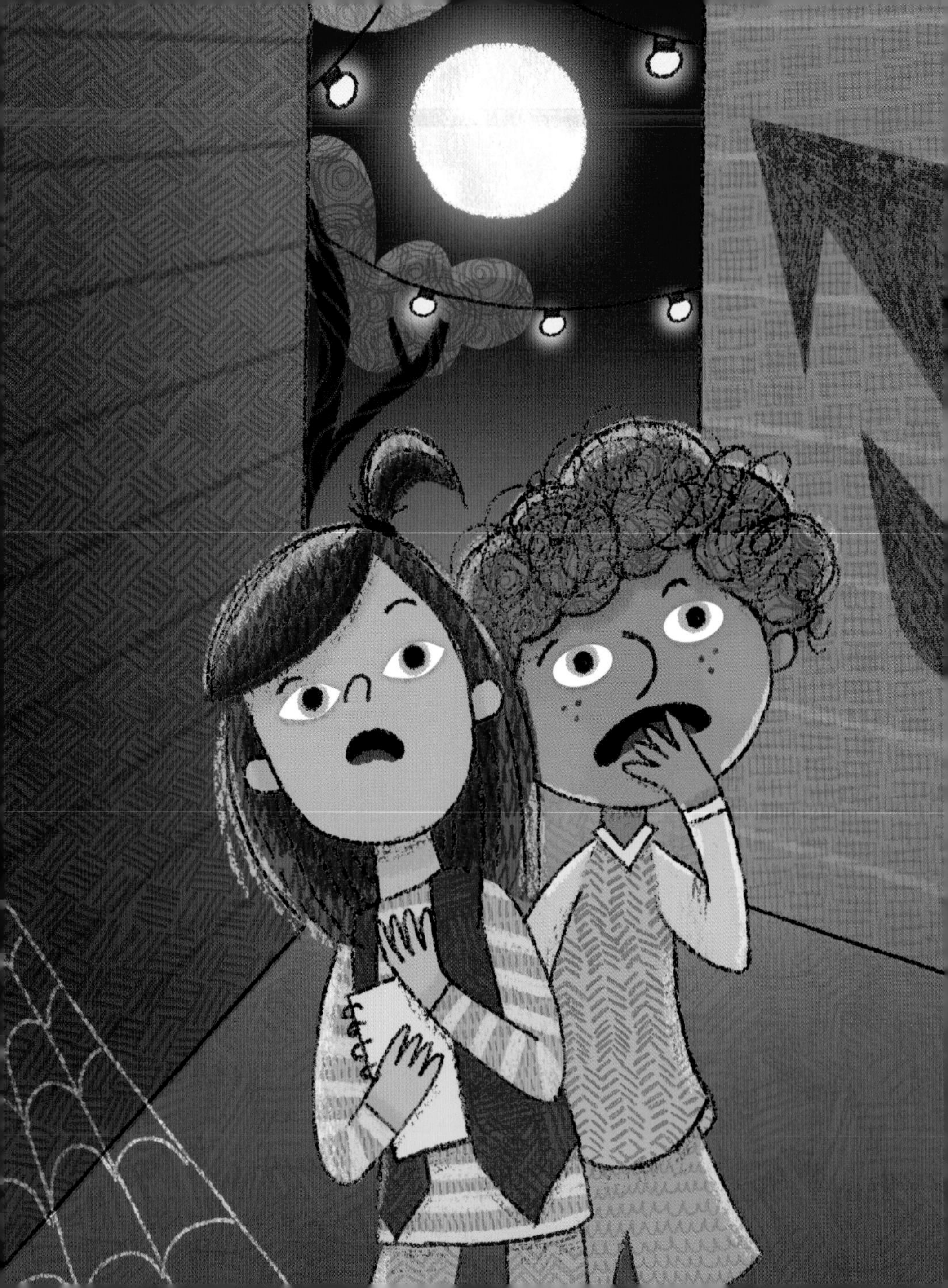

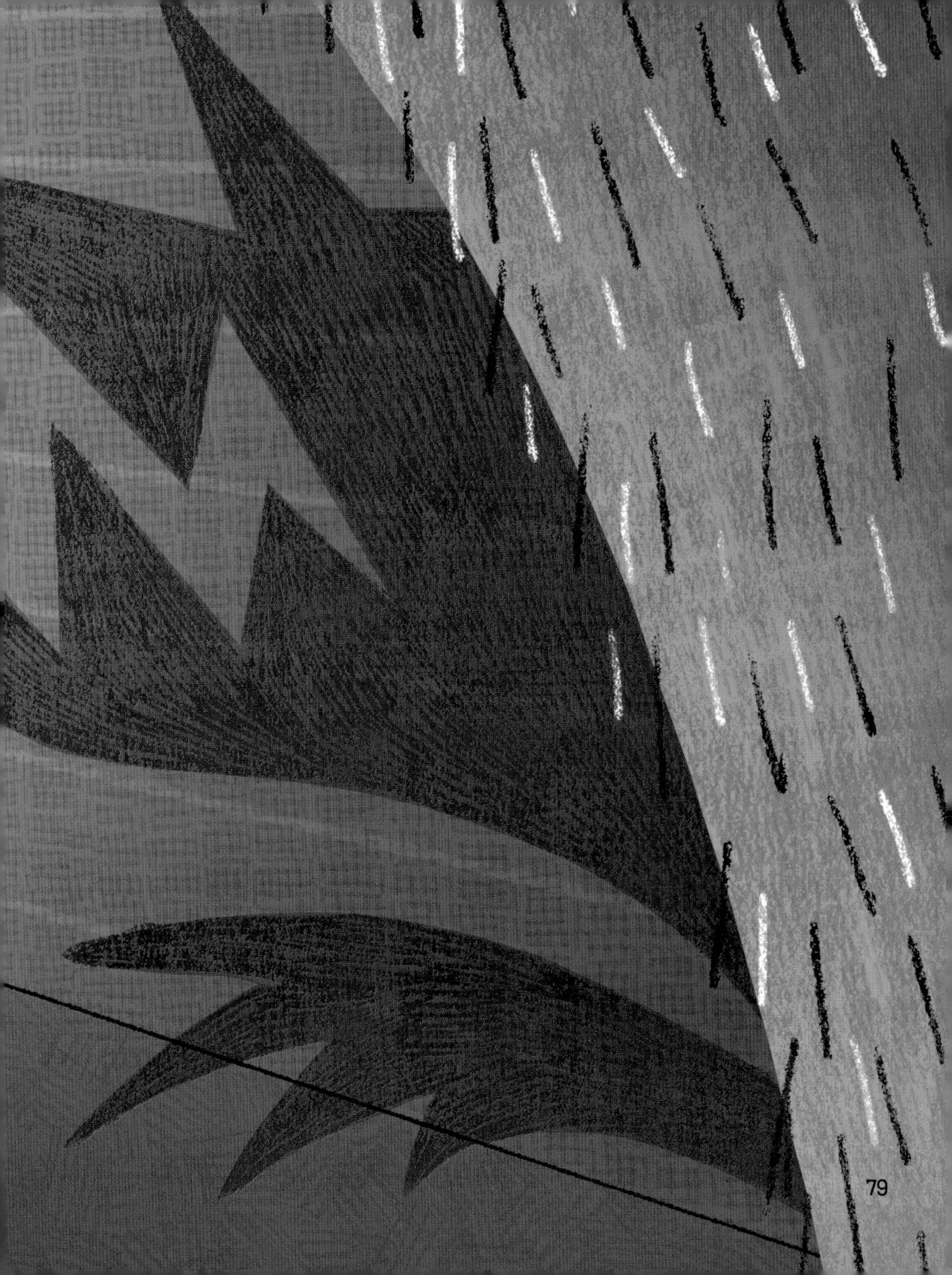

Chapter Seven

I had to catch my breath for a second.

Now, it's true that some facts are scary.

But scary or not, a fact is always a fact.

Fact: The Earth is struck by lightning 100 times per second.

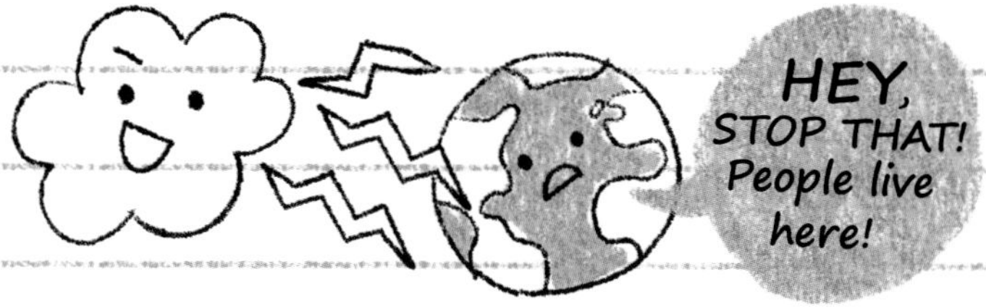
HEY, STOP THAT! People live here!

Fact: The world's largest spider, the giant huntsman, is 12 inches wide—as big as a dinner plate!

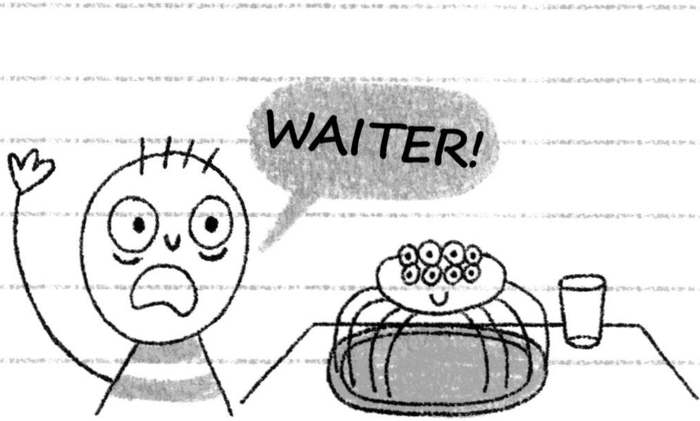
WAITER!

It's also a fact that everything looks scarier in the dark. So maybe what we see is just Fizzle howling at the moon?

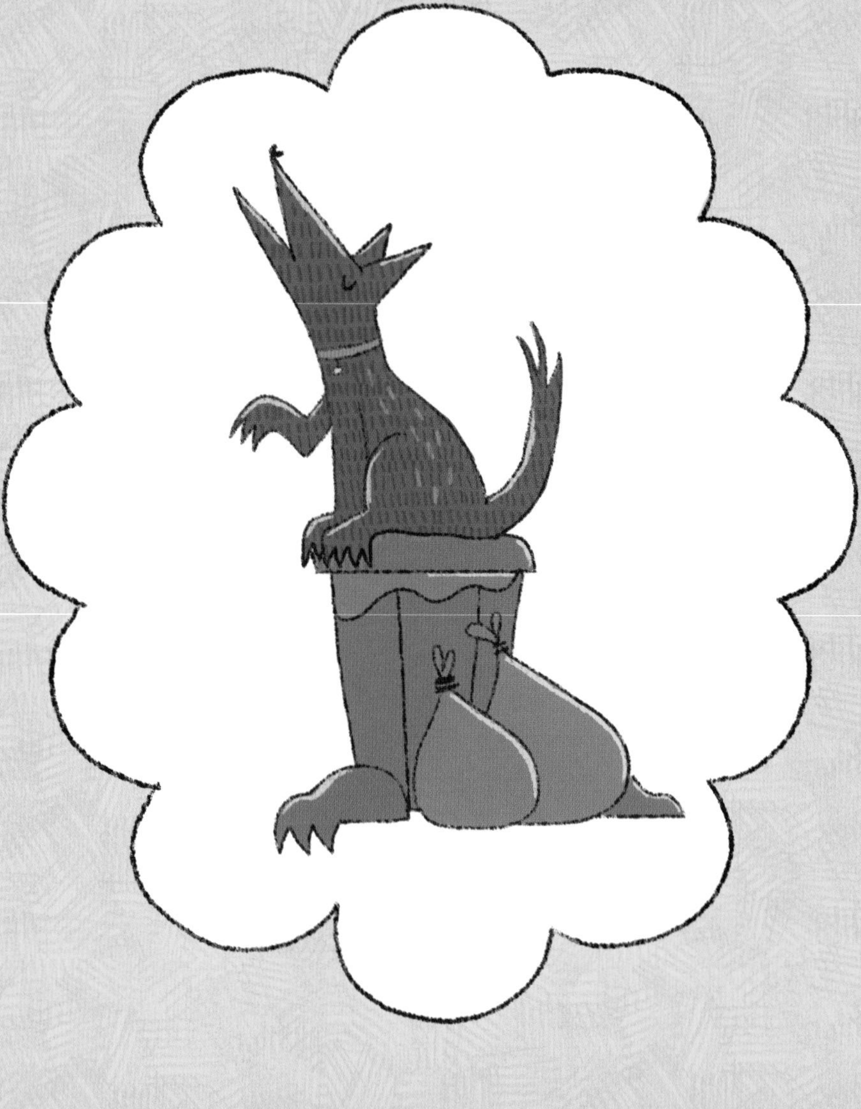

But what if it IS a monster?

HAVE I BEEN PROVEN WRONG?

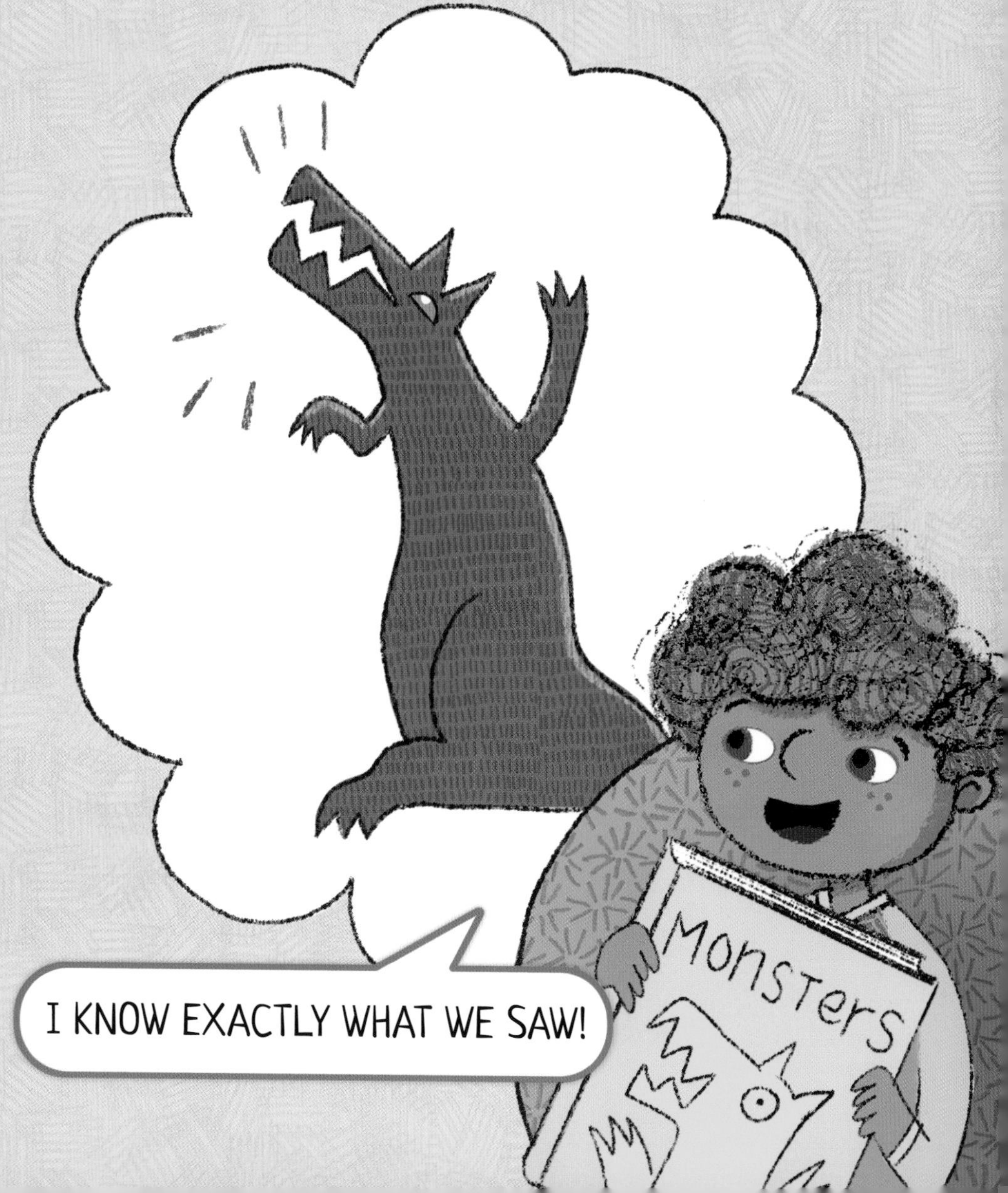
I KNOW EXACTLY WHAT WE SAW!
Monsters

WEREW

A werewolf has two forms, a human form and a wolf form.

In wolf form, werewolves are large beasts covered in thick fur and often have red or yellow eyes.

In human form, appearances vary, but look out for blisters on their hands from walking on all fours.

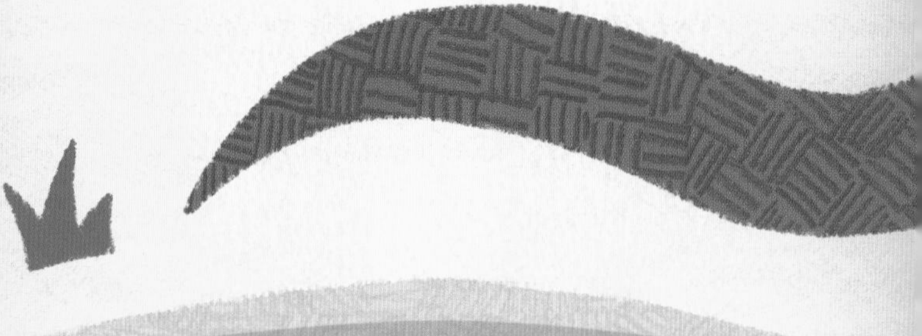

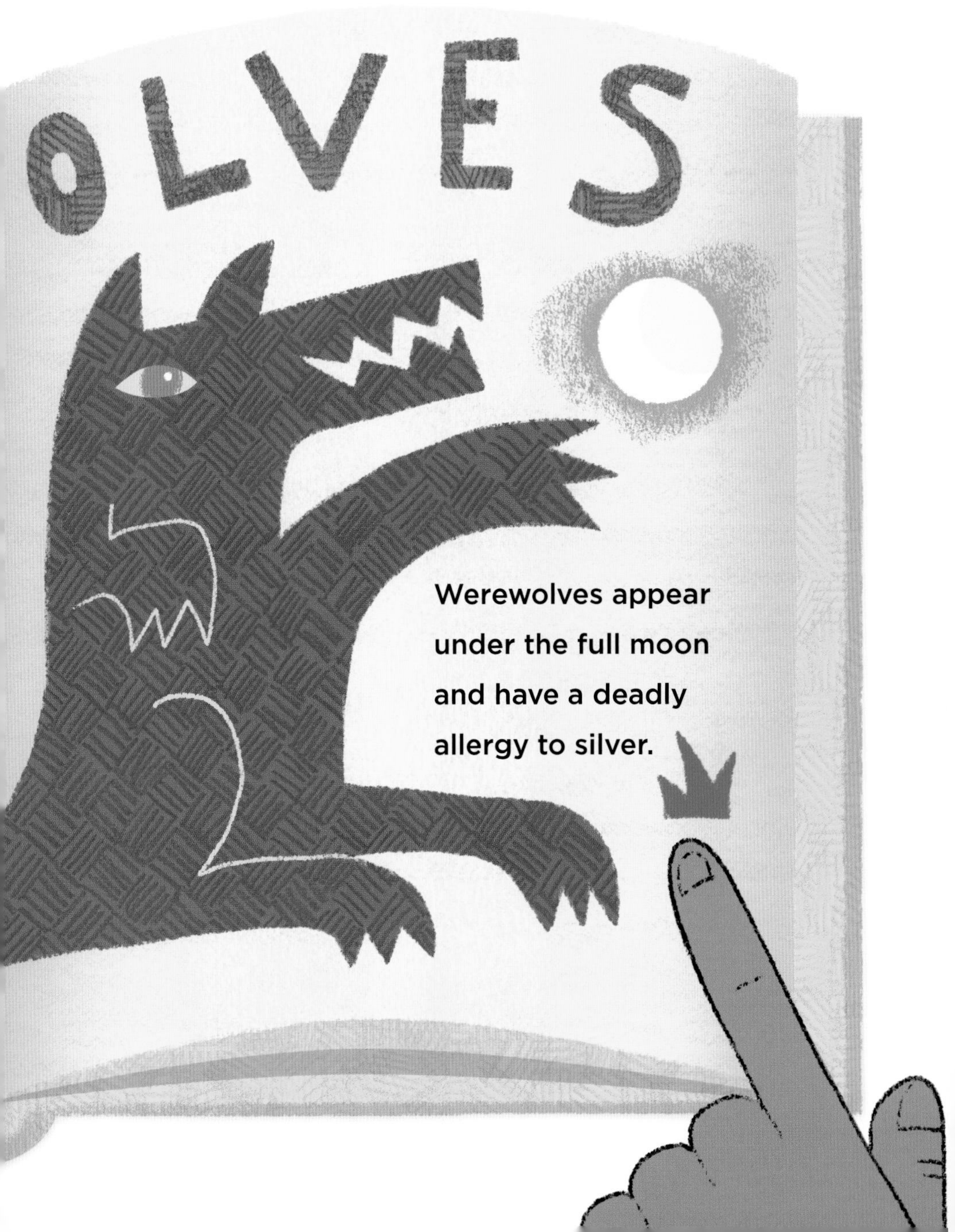
OLVES

Werewolves appear under the full moon and have a deadly allergy to silver.

After a fact is proven, NEW evidence might show up!

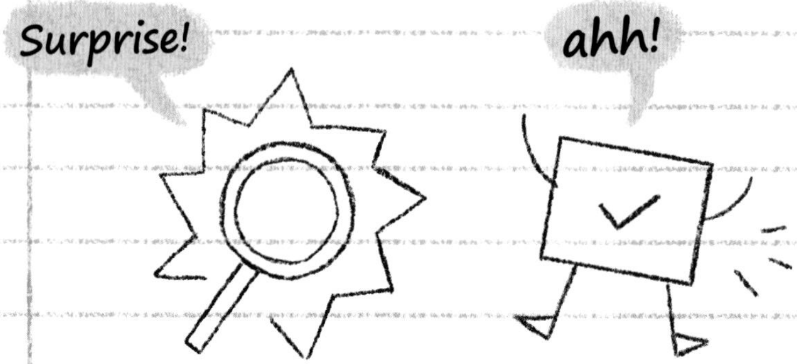
Surprise!
ahh!

This means facts can change, so you need to prove them again.

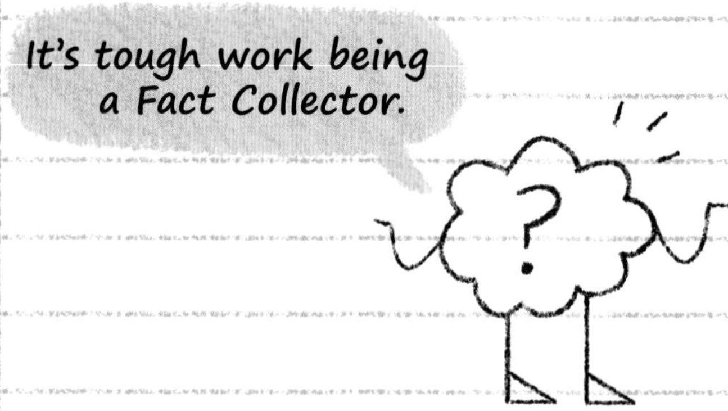
It's tough work being a Fact Collector.

And even though Penn's monster book is a book of fiction, could it be pointing to an unproven fact?

Is there a werewolf on Evergreen Street?

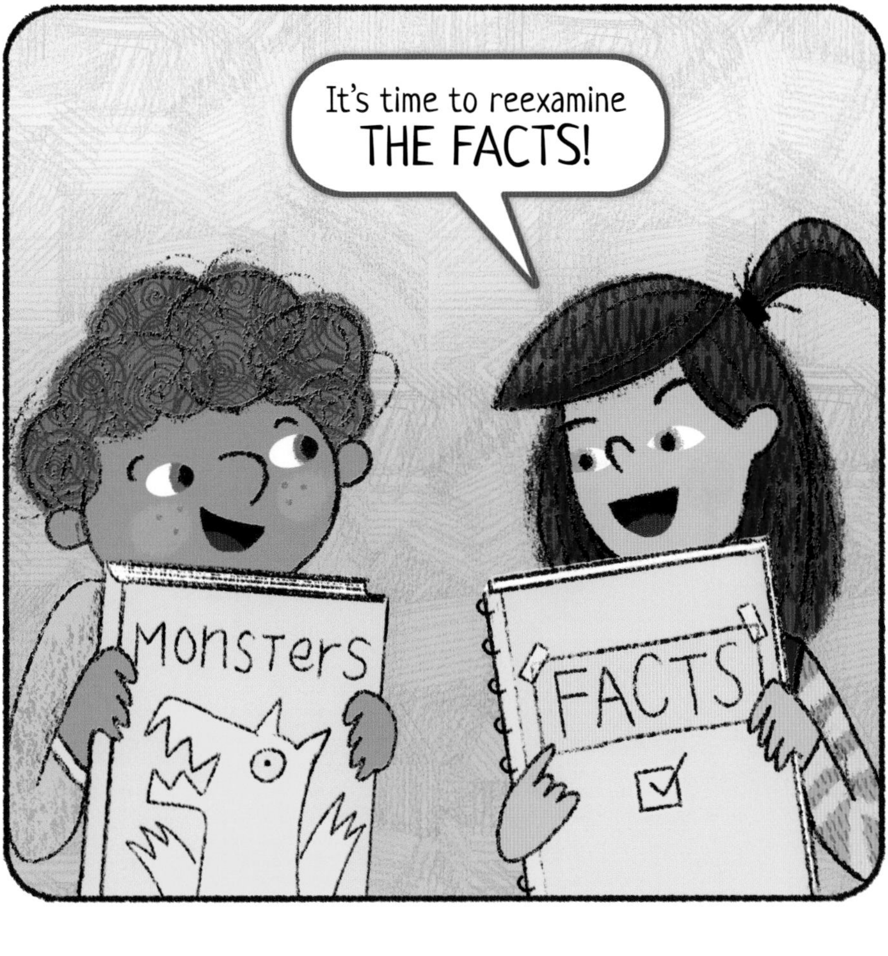
It's time to reexamine THE FACTS!
Monsters
FACTS

Chapter Eight

Fact: a number of humans live on Evergreen Street.

Guess: one of them might be a . . . werewolf!

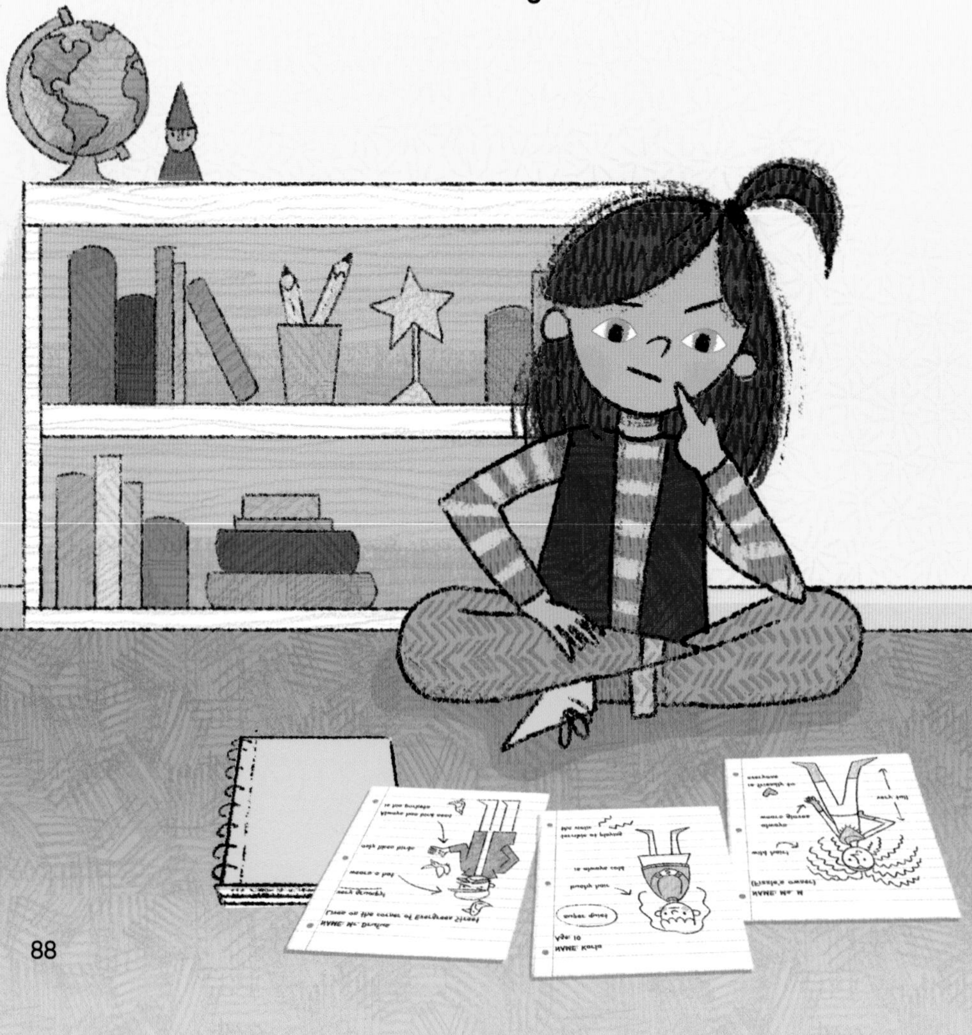

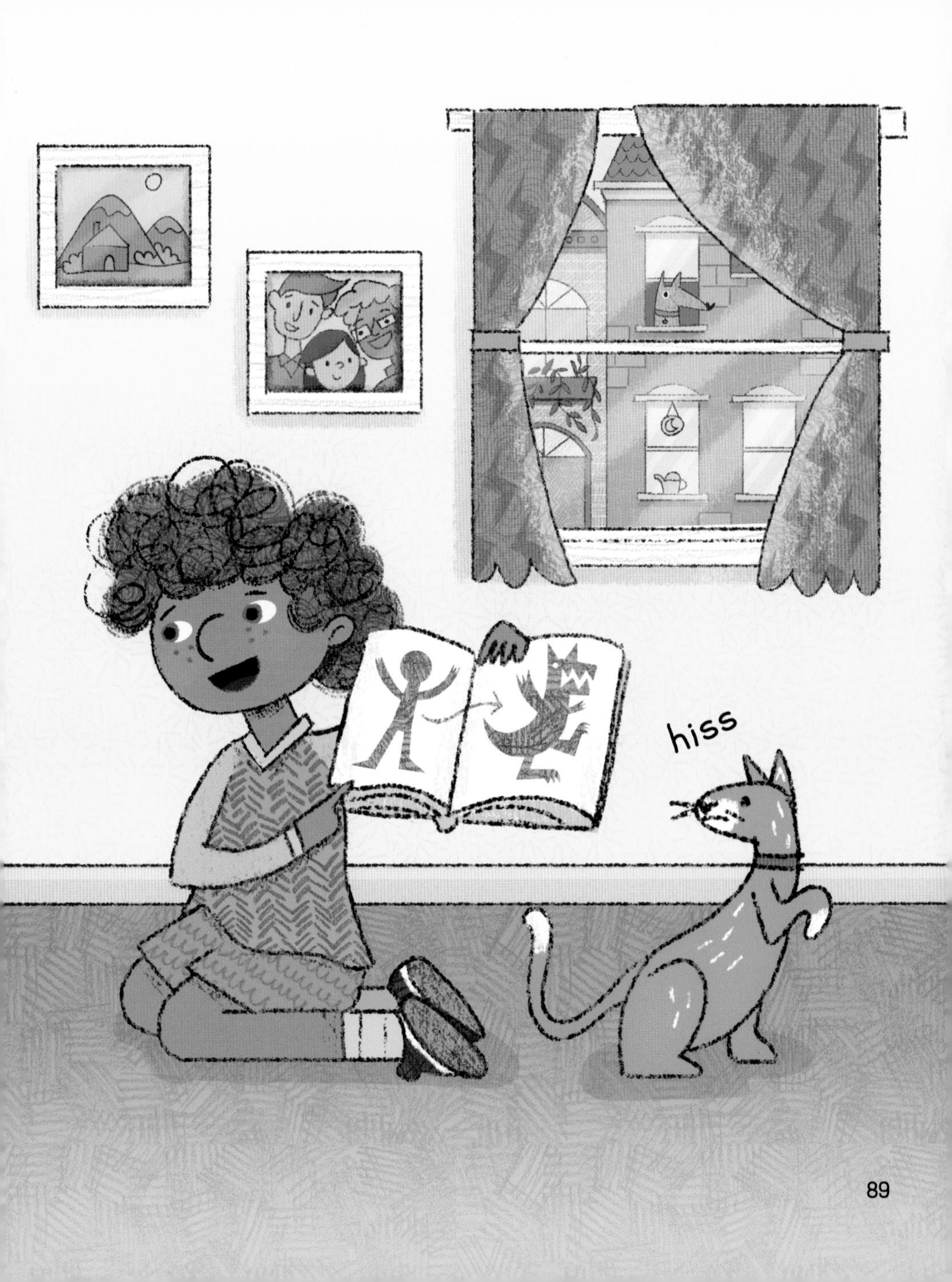
hiss

What about Mr. Drufus? He's so grumpy! He could be the werewolf!

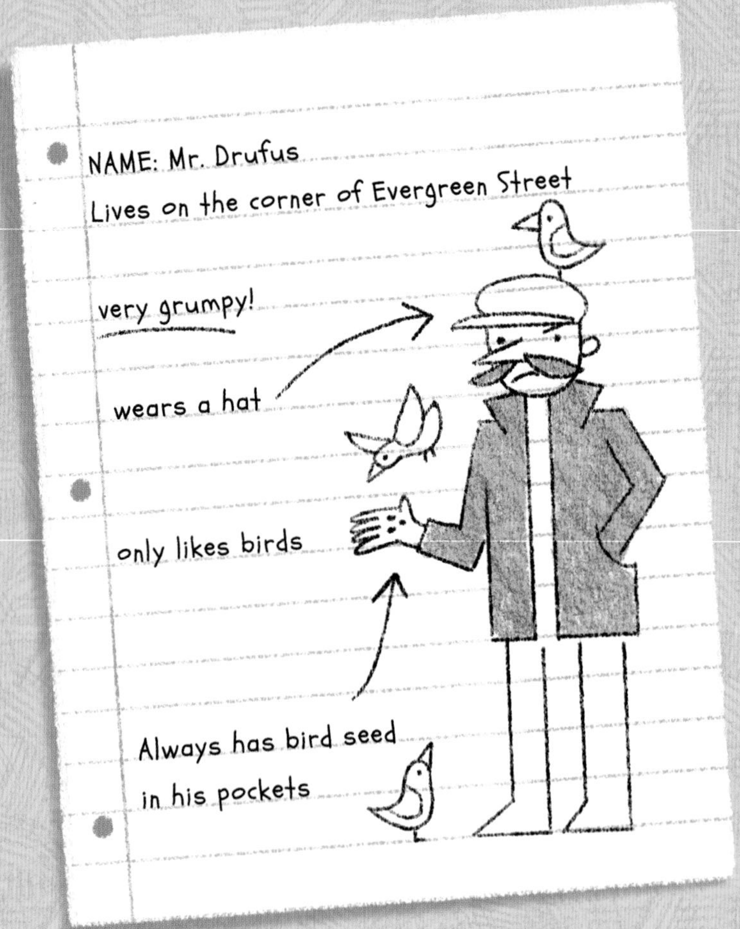
NAME: Mr. Drufus
Lives on the corner of Evergreen Street
very grumpy!
wears a hat
only likes birds
Always has bird seed
in his pockets

No. Remember we saw him at the Full Moon Festival complaining about the hot cocoa?

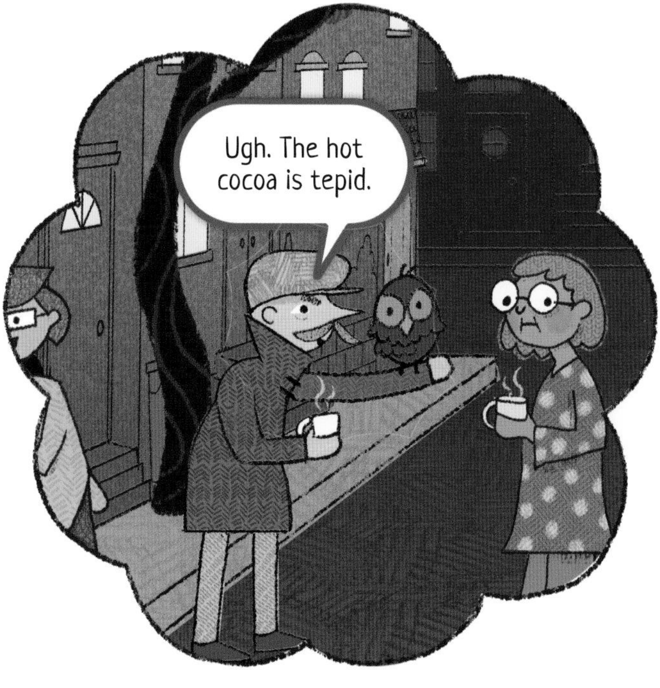
Ugh. The hot cocoa is tepid.

Oh right! Eh, he's too bald to be a werewolf anyway.

What about Karla? She's quiet . . .
maybe she's hiding something?

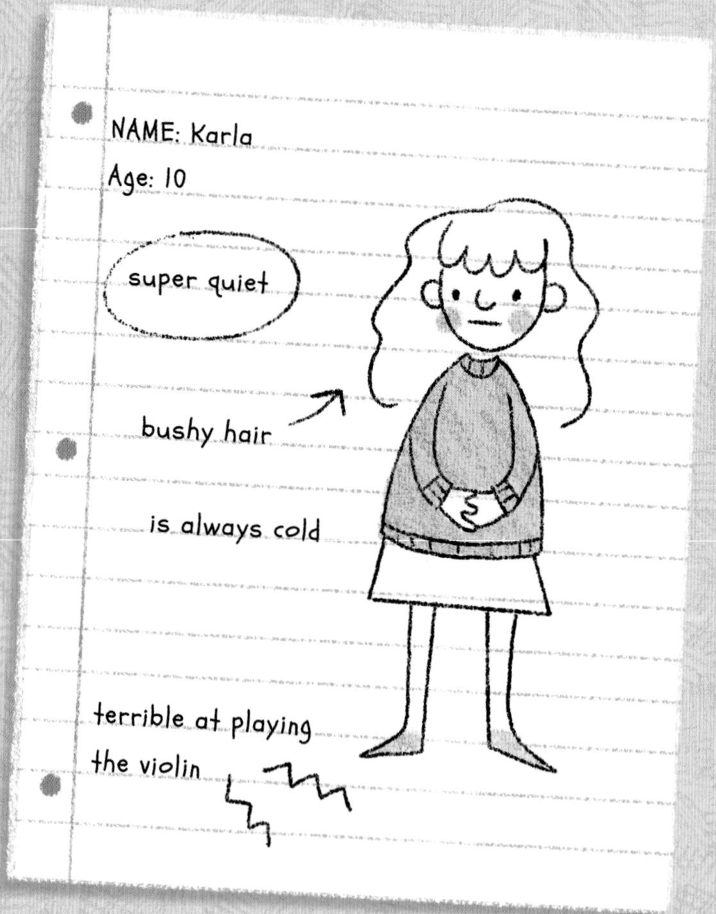

False. I recall seeing her at the festival, talking to the kid with the pet rock.

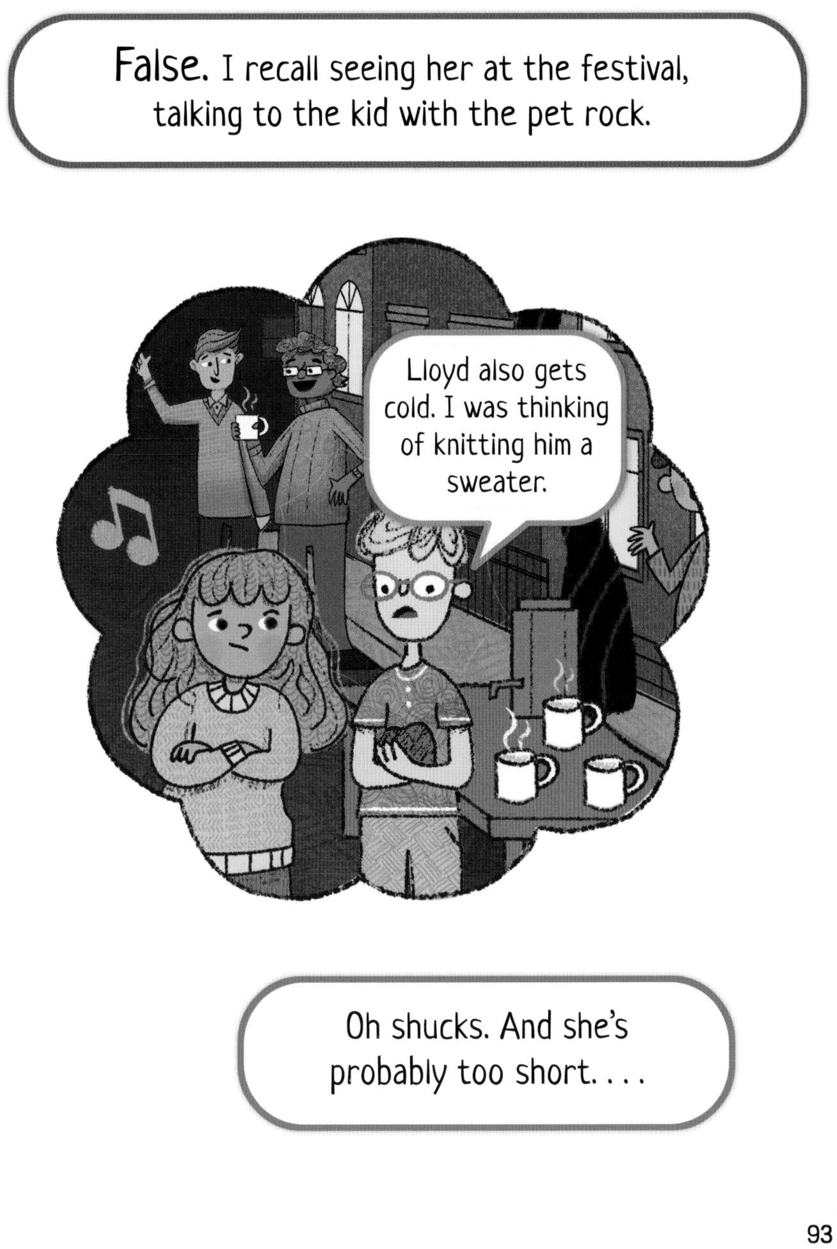
Lloyd also gets cold. I was thinking of knitting him a sweater.

Oh shucks. And she's probably too short. . . .

What about Ms. M? I don't remember seeing her at the Full Moon Festival.

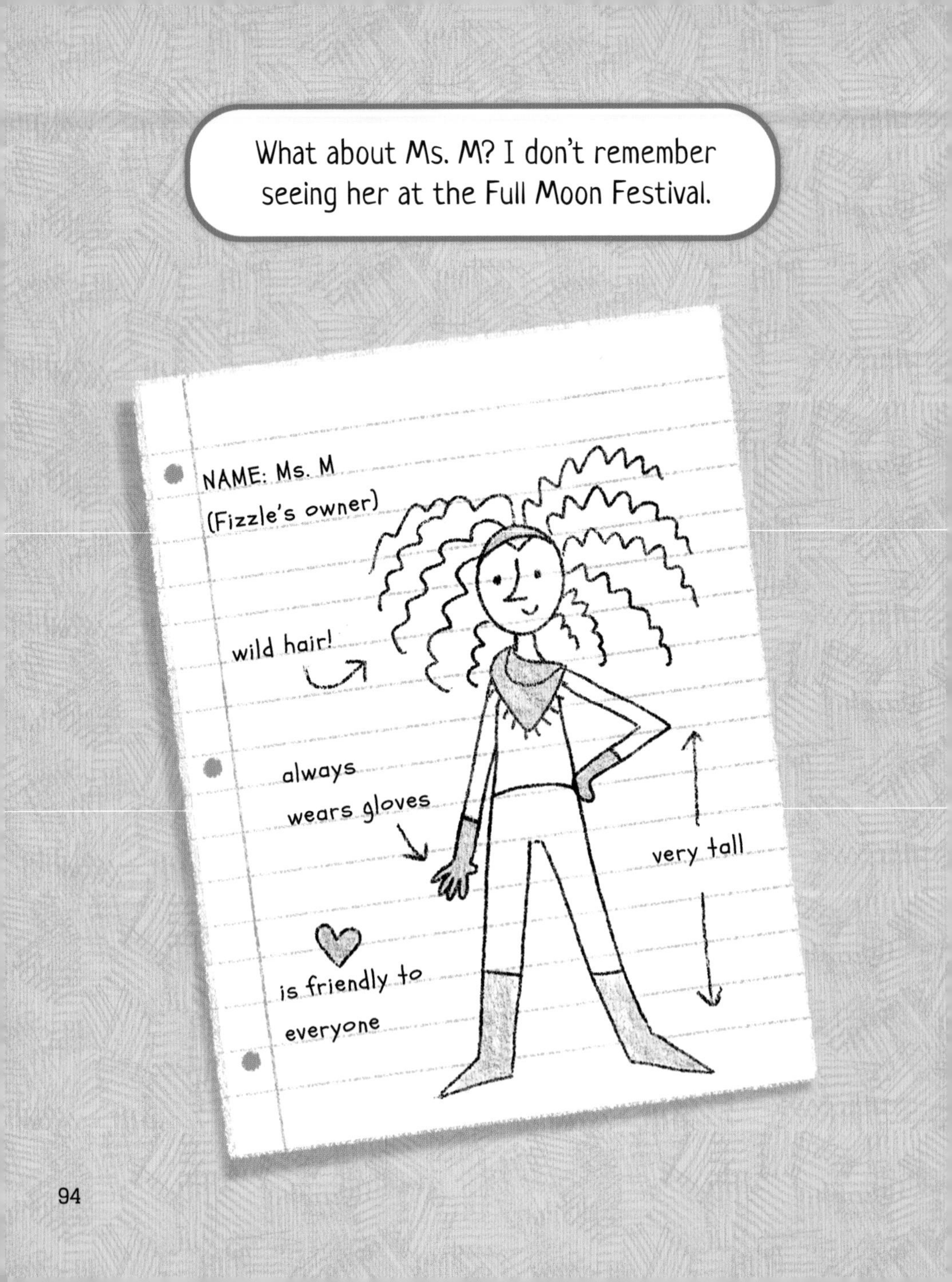
NAME: Ms. M
(Fizzle's owner)
wild hair!
always wears gloves
very tall
is friendly to everyone

But she's so nice!

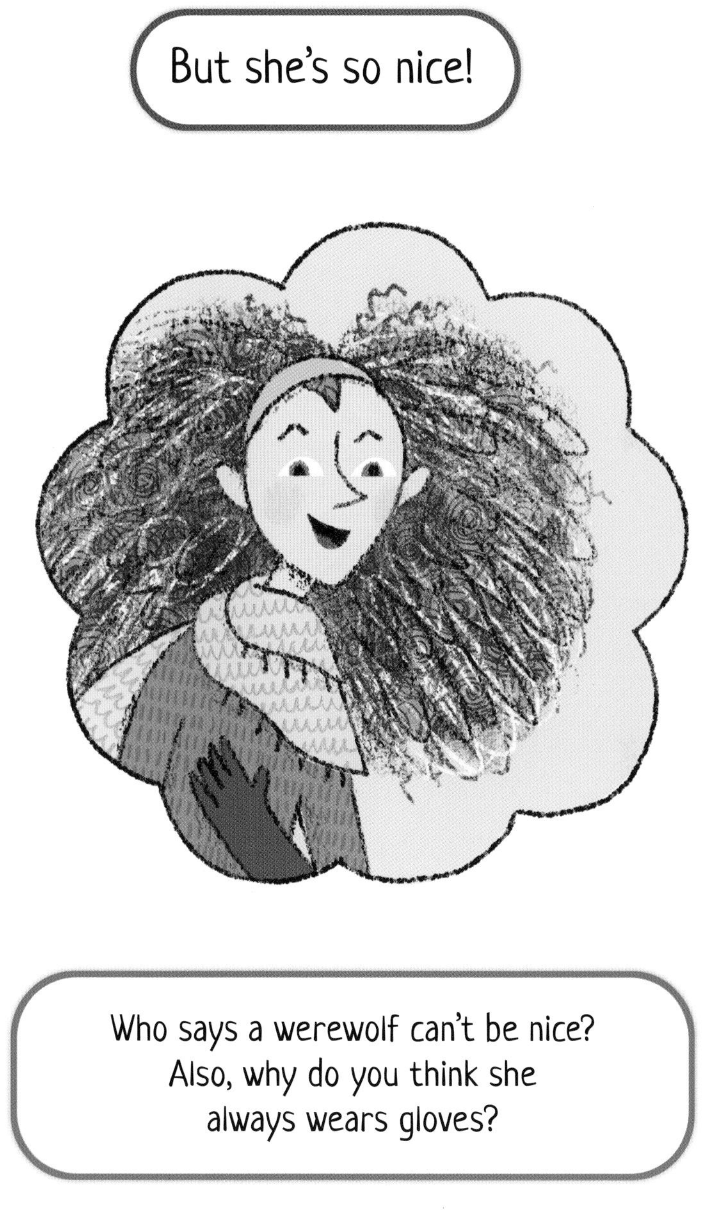

Who says a werewolf can't be nice?
Also, why do you think she
always wears gloves?

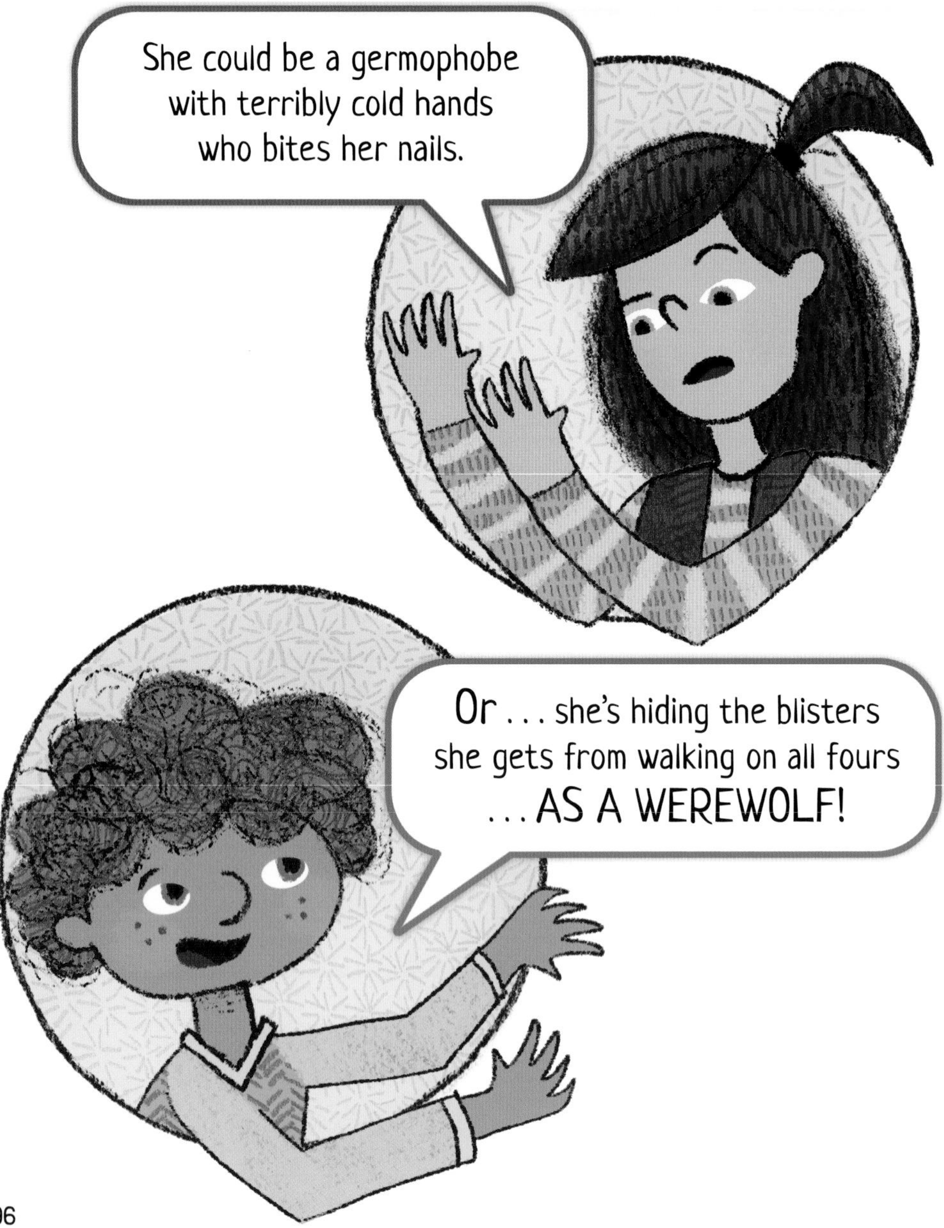
She could be a germophobe with terribly cold hands who bites her nails.
Or . . . she's hiding the blisters she gets from walking on all fours . . . AS A WEREWOLF!

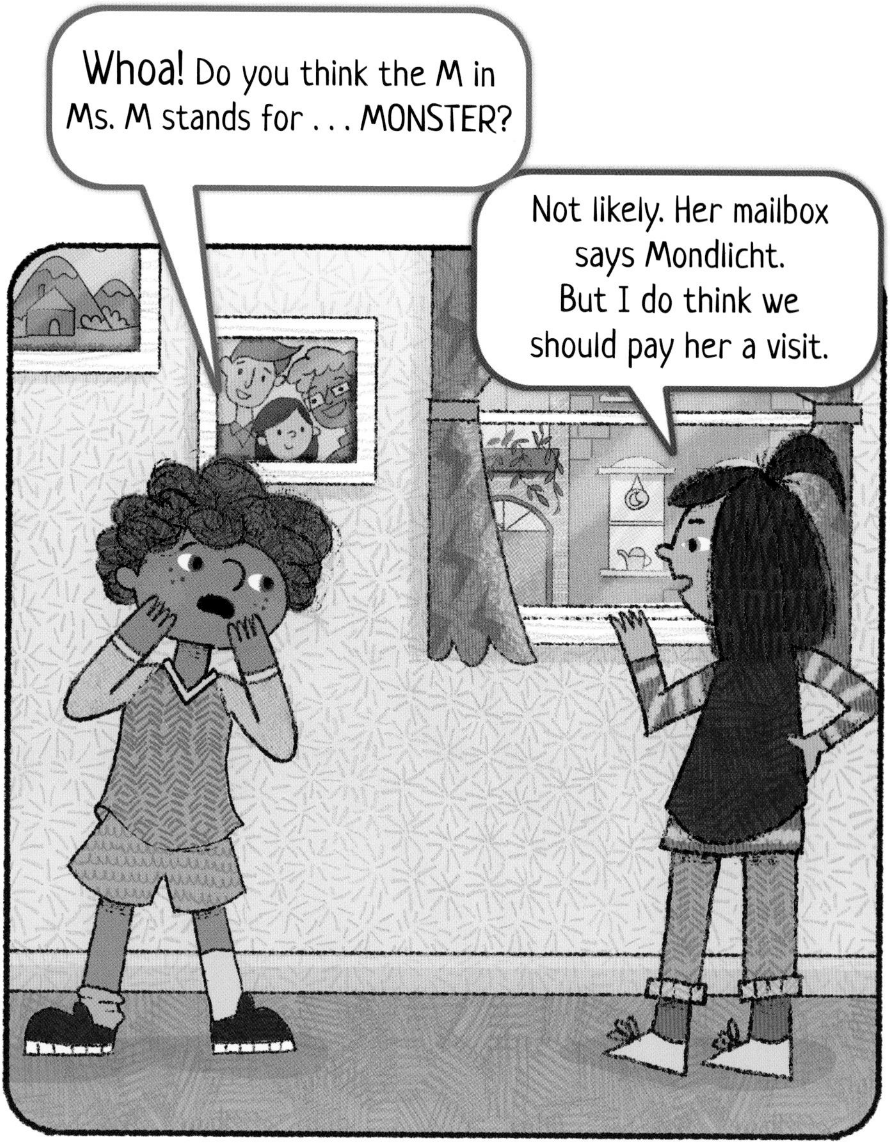
Whoa! Do you think the M in Ms. M stands for . . . MONSTER?
Not likely. Her mailbox says Mondlicht. But I do think we should pay her a visit.

Chapter Nine

One of the best ways to check evidence is to go to the source: That's right, Ms. M.'s house.

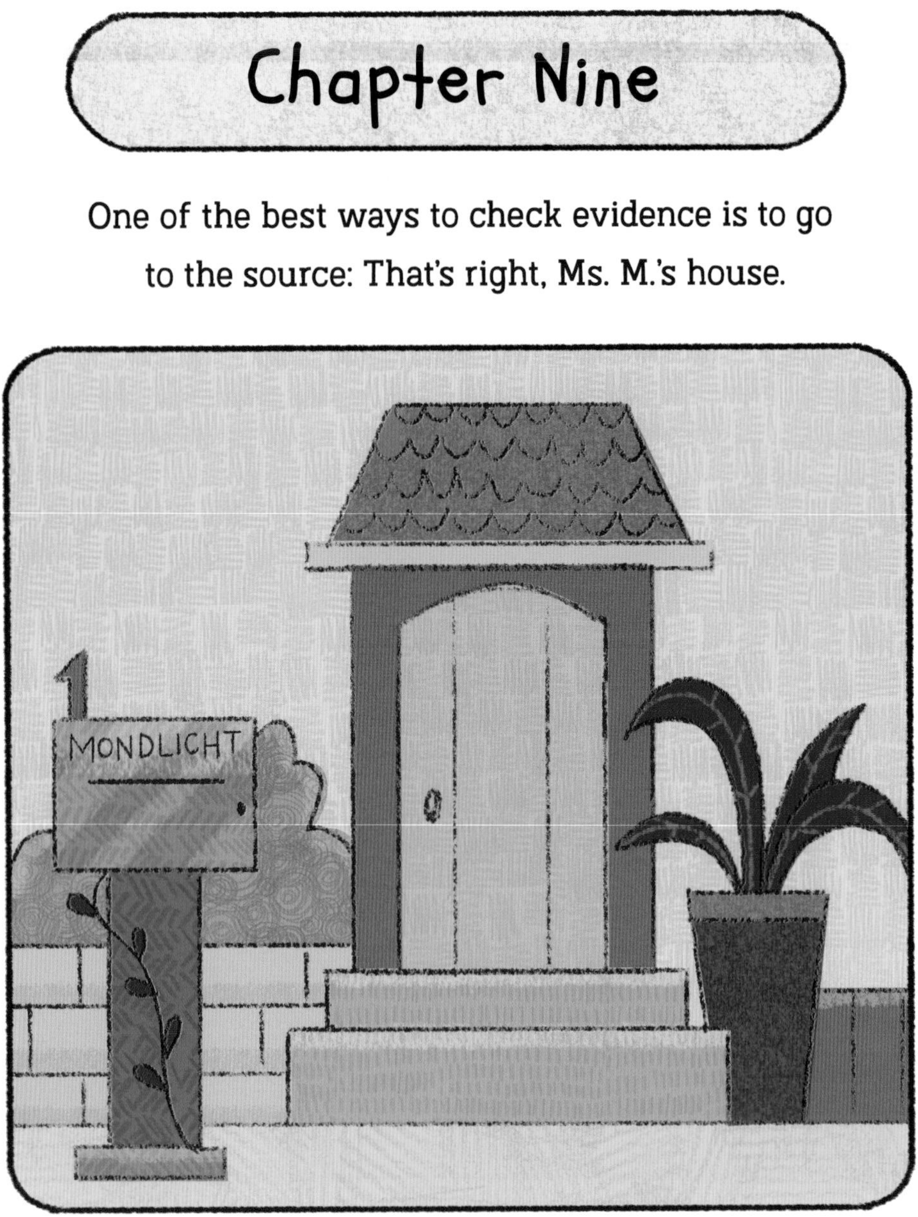
1
MONDLICHT

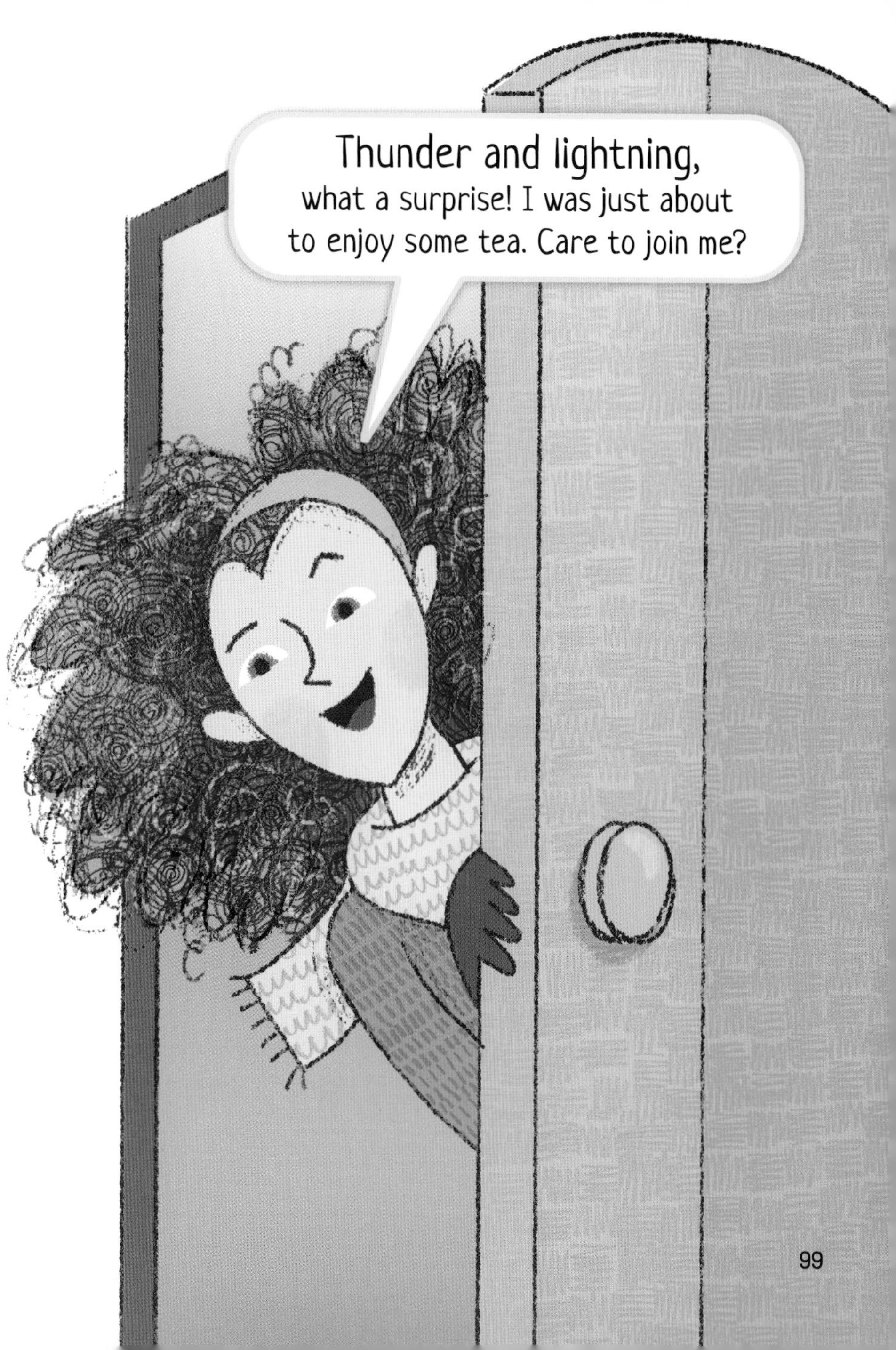
Thunder and lightning, what a surprise! I was just about to enjoy some tea. Care to join me?

Ms. M's home doesn't look like the home of a werewolf. But then again, I've never been to the home of a werewolf . . . that I know of.

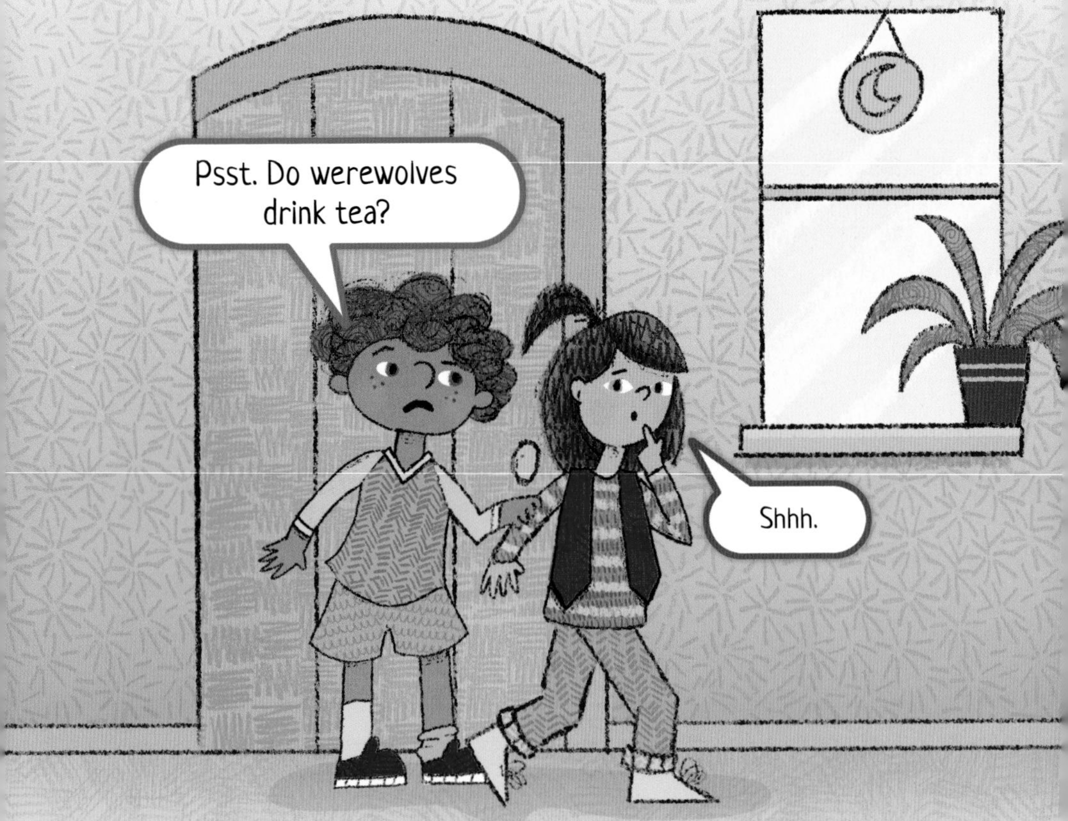
Psst. Do werewolves drink tea?
Shhh.

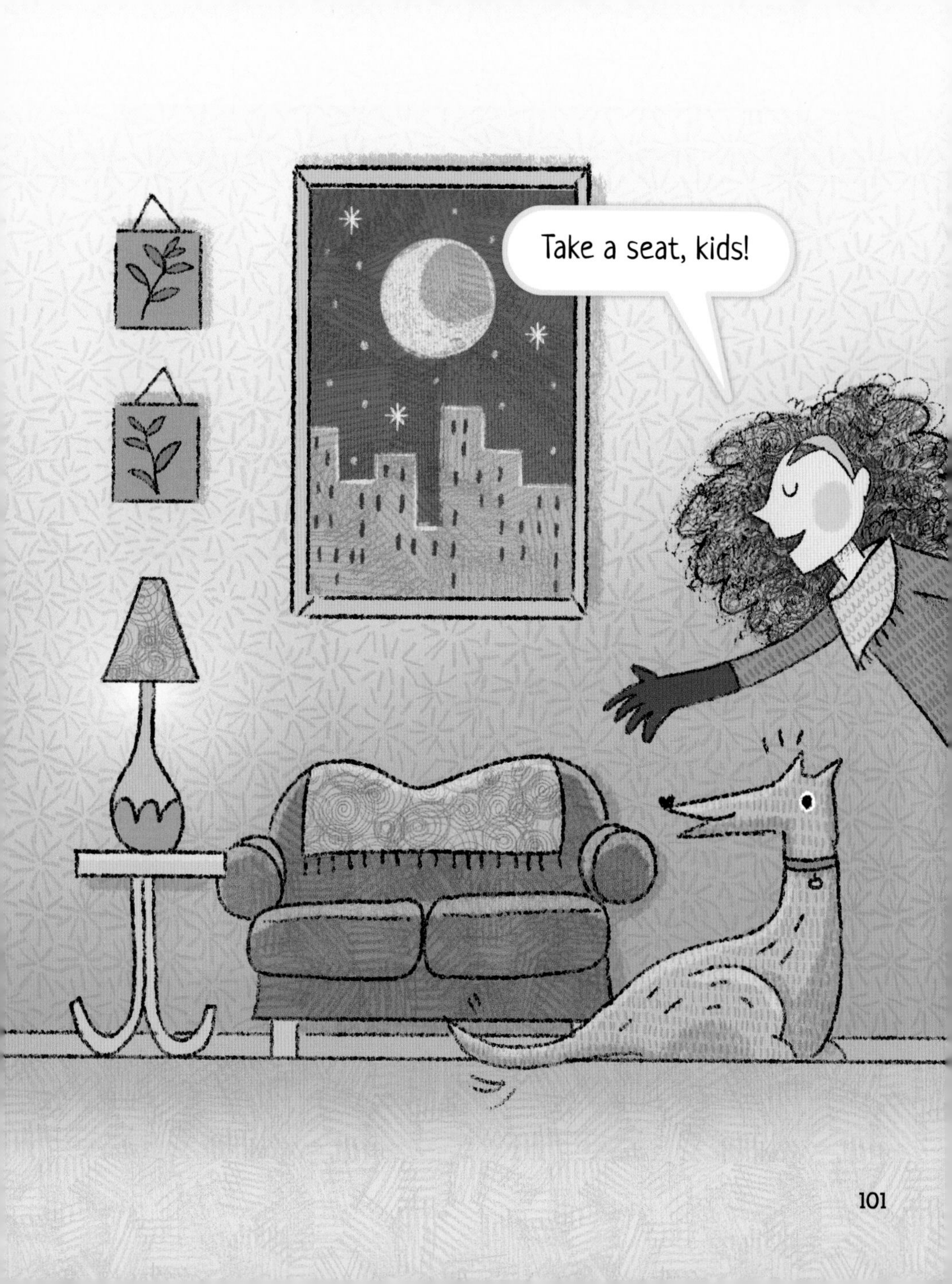
Take a seat, kids!

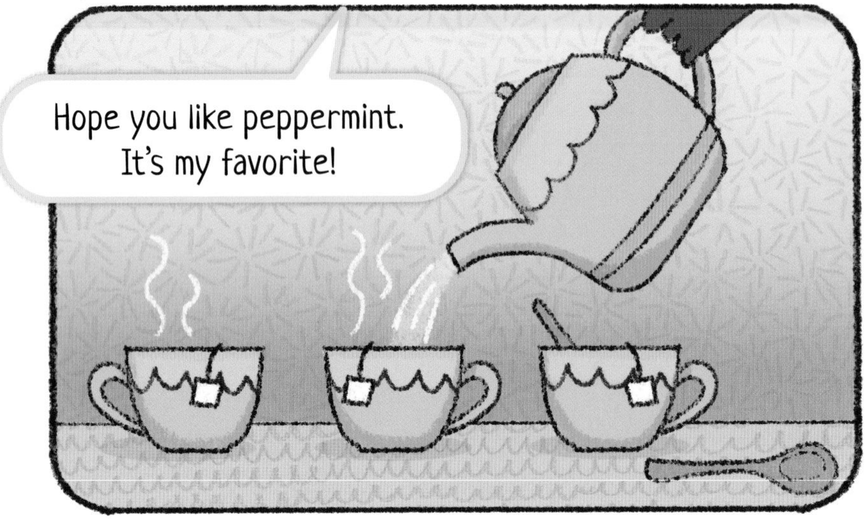
Hope you like peppermint. It's my favorite!

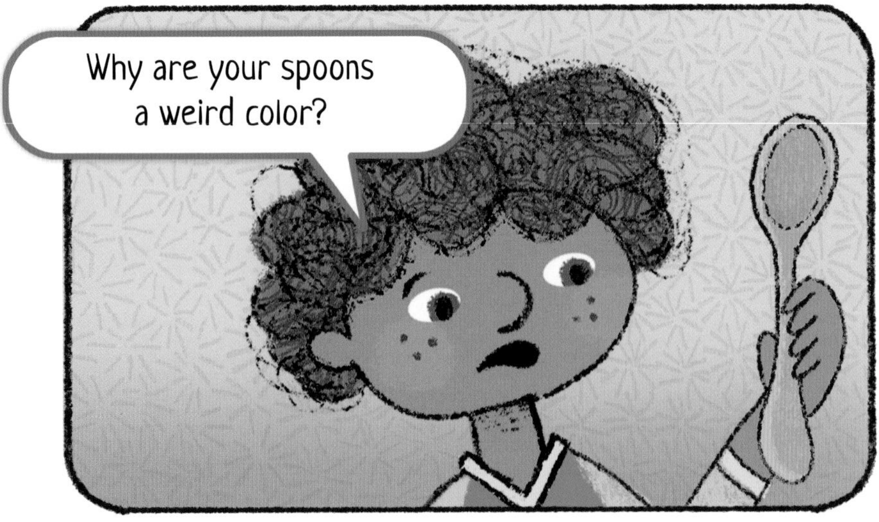
Why are your spoons a weird color?

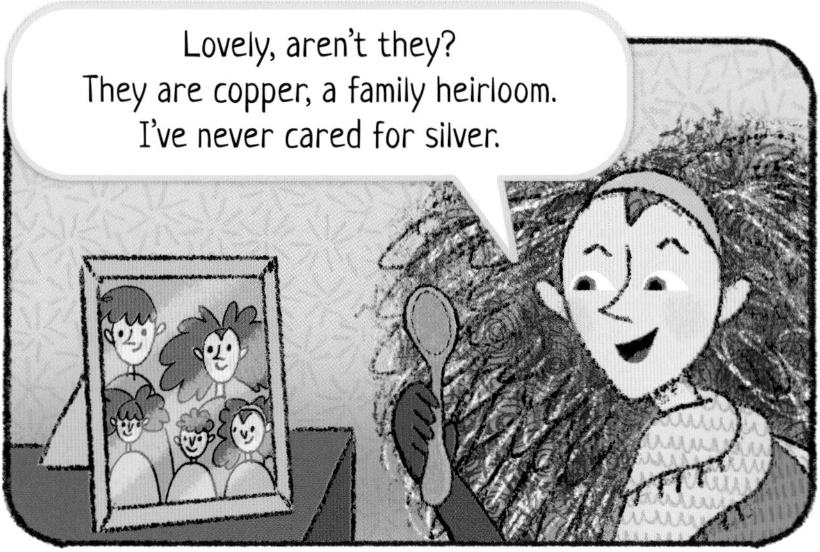
Lovely, aren't they? They are copper, a family heirloom. I've never cared for silver.

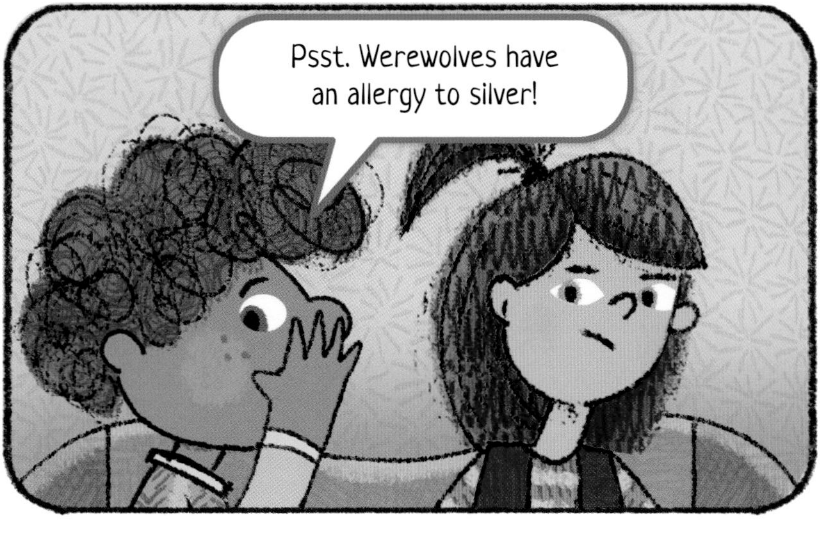
Psst. Werewolves have an allergy to silver!

I couldn't wait one more second!

I had a question that needed an answer.

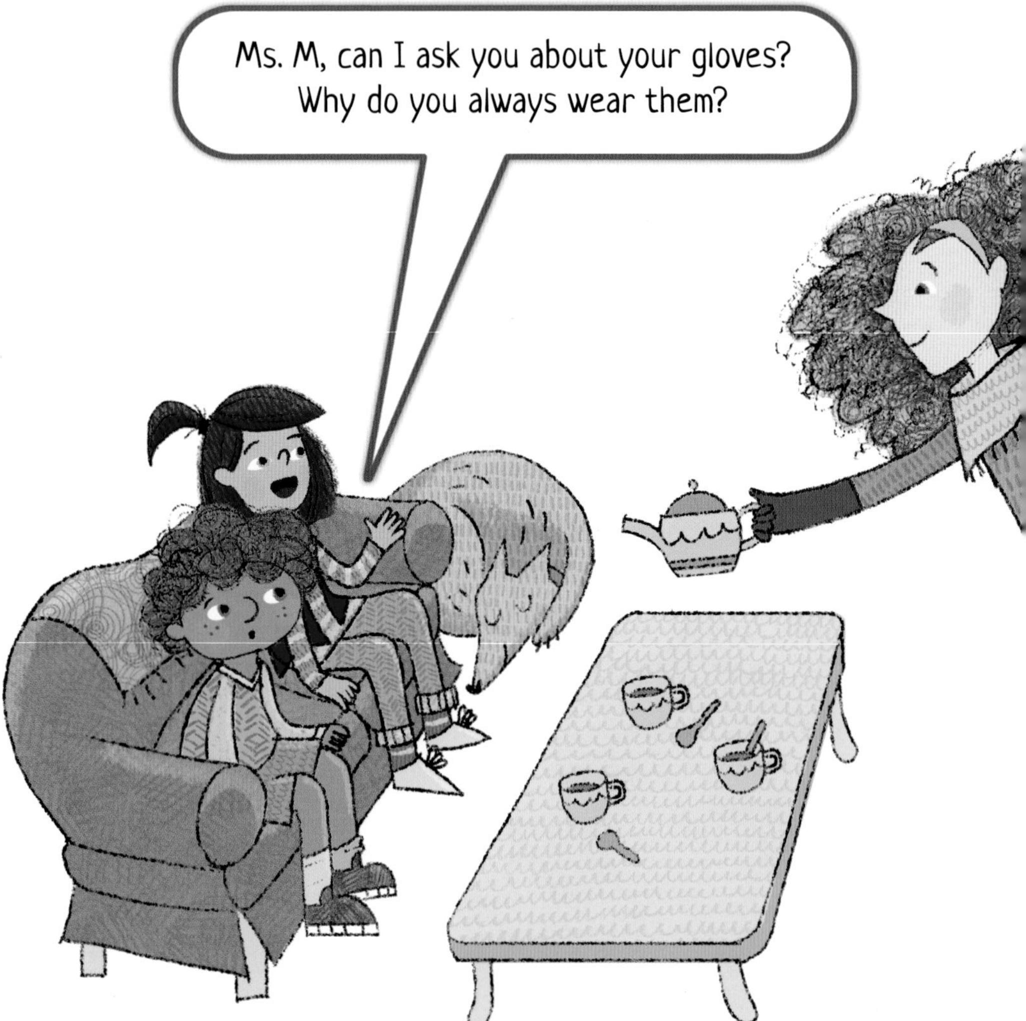
Ms. M, can I ask you about your gloves? Why do you always wear them?

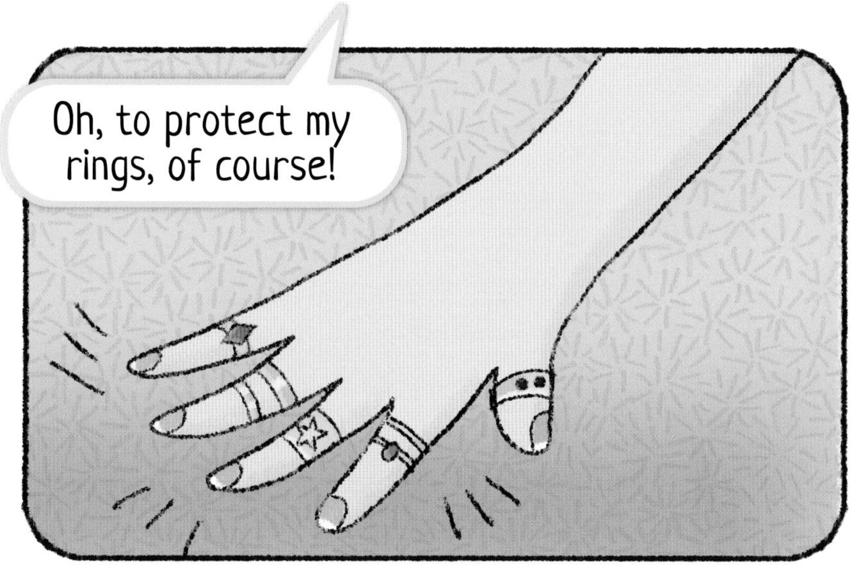
Oh, to protect my rings, of course!

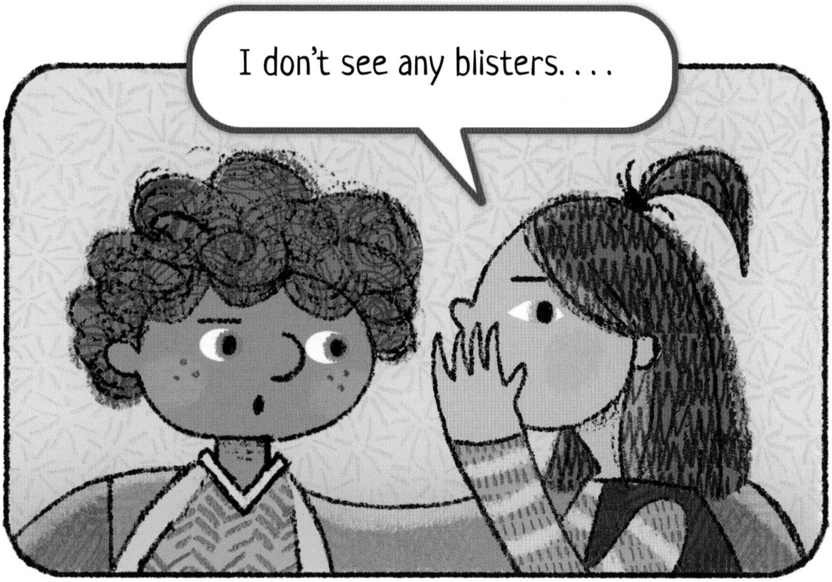
I don't see any blisters. . . .

It is time to get to the truth, once and for all.

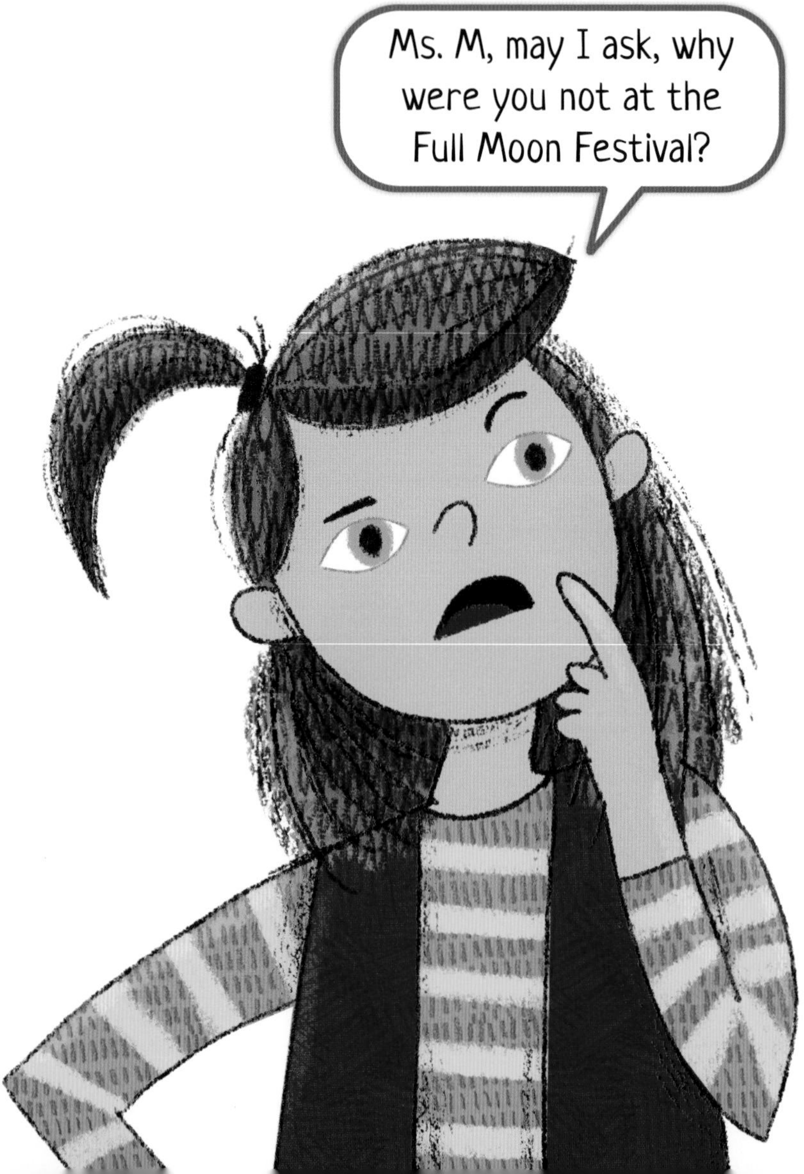
Ms. M, may I ask, why were you not at the Full Moon Festival?

At first Ms. M didn't say a word.
No one said a word.

But then she told us what really happened.

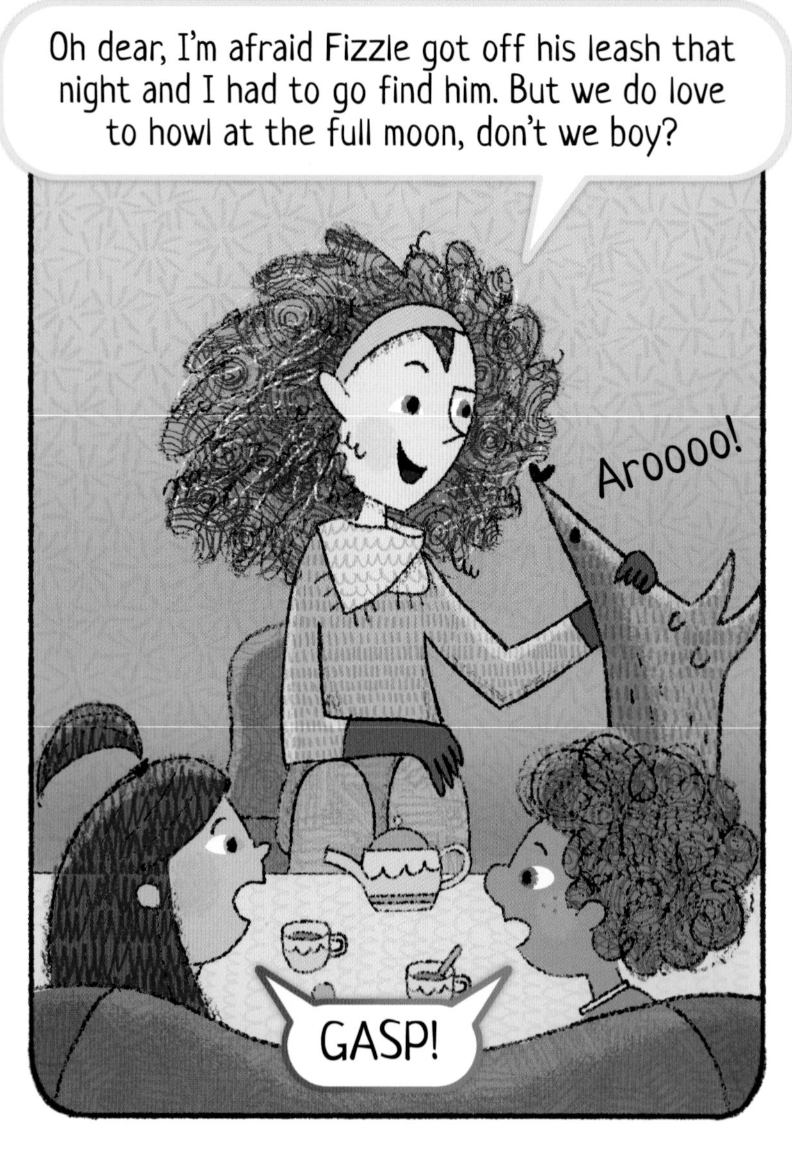
Oh dear, I'm afraid Fizzle got off his leash that night and I had to go find him. But we do love to howl at the full moon, don't we boy?
Aroooo!
GASP!

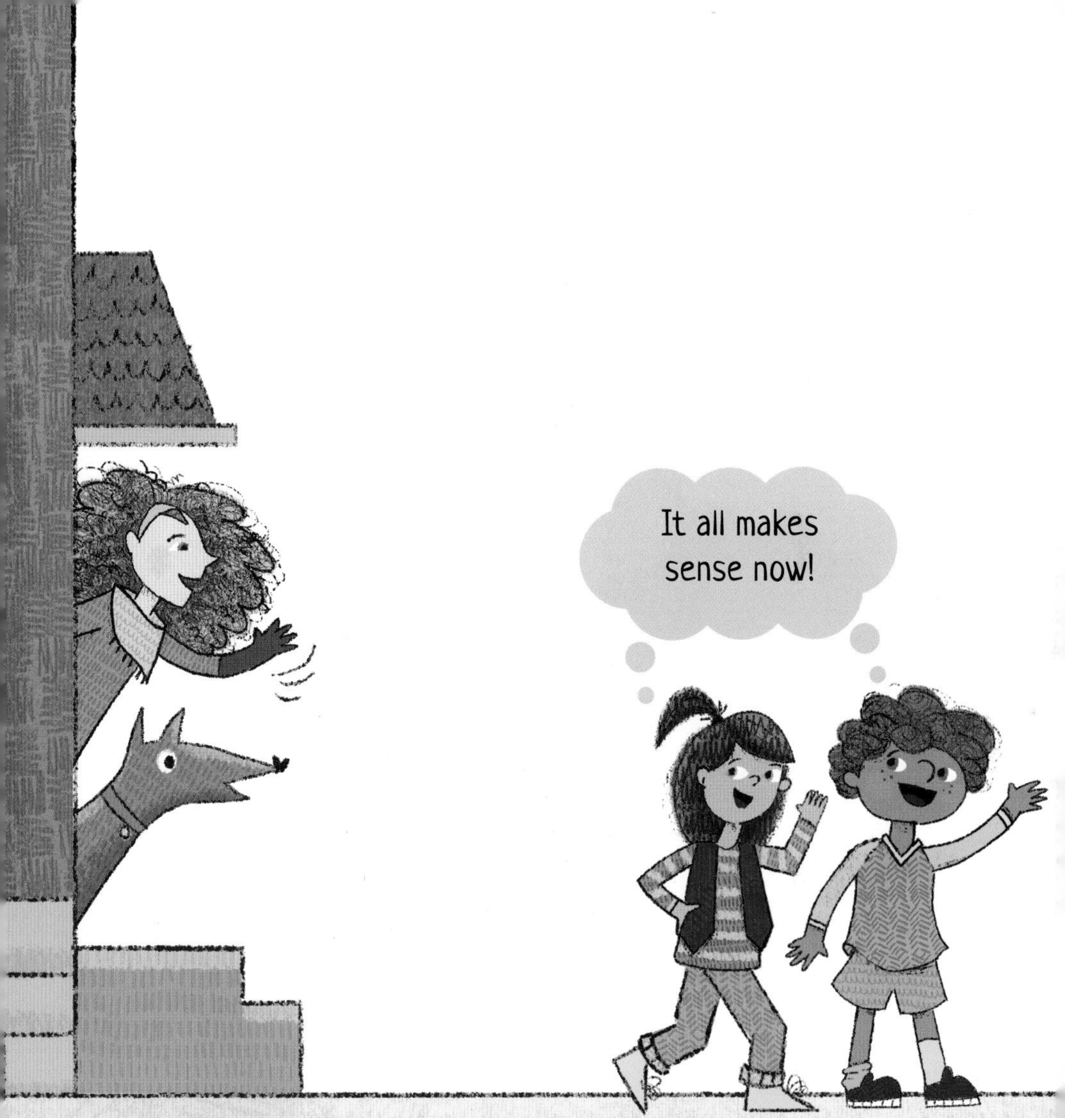
It all makes sense now!

The fact is that sometimes two different people look at the exact same facts and. . .

have two different conclusions.

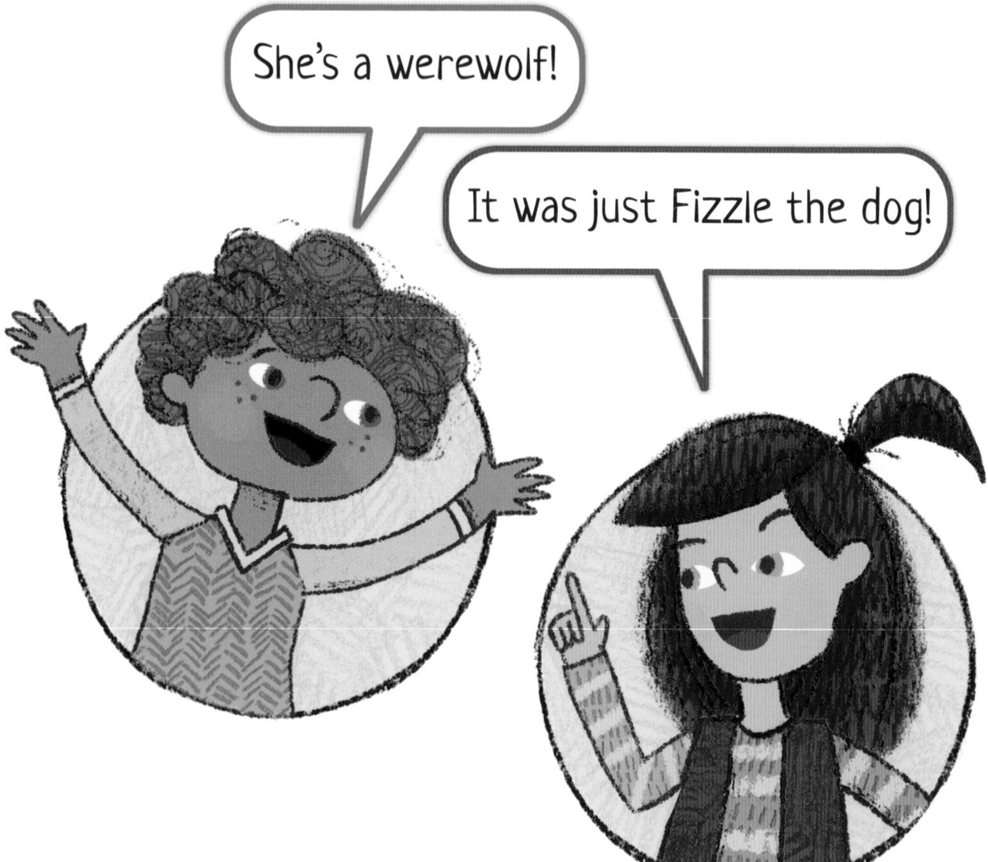
She's a werewolf!
It was just Fizzle the dog!

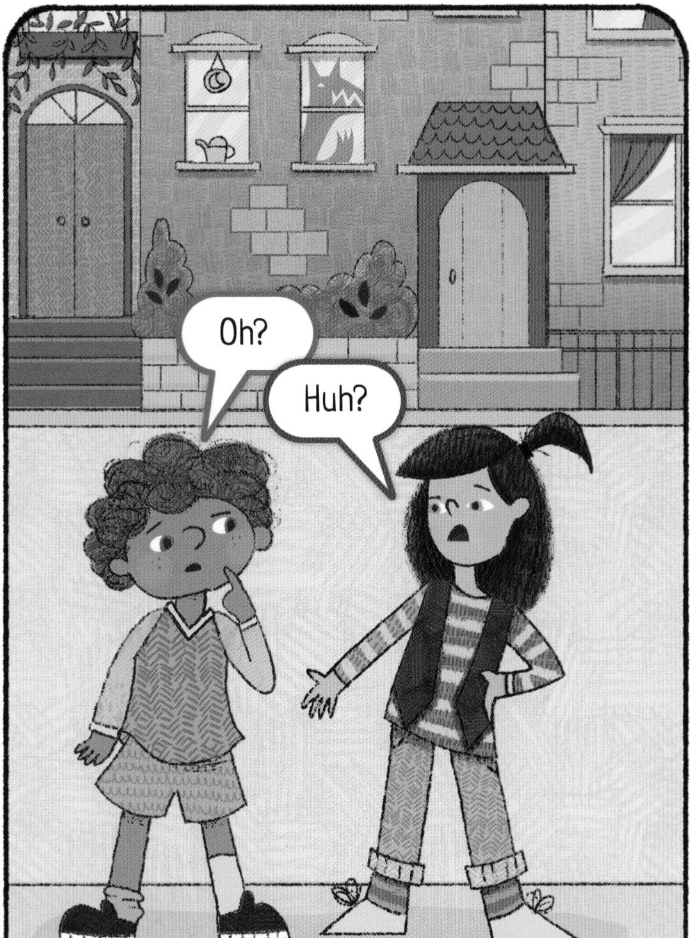
Oh?
Huh?

And that is the real mystery!

Is there a werewolf monster on Evergreen Street?

Or a dog that likes to howl at the moon?

To me, the facts are clear.

Penn and I might not agree,
but there is one thing we DO agree on.

Fact: We are friends!

Yes! So, let me tell you about this ghost I saw once. . . .